24 GUN CONTROL PLAYS

By

Elaine Avila, Neil Blackadder, Kyle Bostian,
Alex Broun, Gab Cody,
Tameka Cage Conley, Cecilia Copeland,
Amina Henry, Yvette Heyliger, Zac Kline,
Neil LaBute, Jennifer Maisel,
Lynn Manning, Oliver Mayer,
Chiori Miyagawa, Winter Miller,
Matthew Paul Olmos, Ian Rowlands,
August Schulenburg, Saviana Stanescu,
Caridad Svich, Chris Weikel, Gary Winter and
Laura Zam

With an essay by Tammy Ryan
And a reflection and interview
By D.W. Gregory .

Curated and edited by
Caridad Svich and Zac Kline

NoPassport Press
Dreaming the Americas Series

NoPassport Press
Dreaming the Americas Series
PO Box 1786, South Gate CA 90280 USA;
NoPassportPress@aol.com
www.nopassport.org

ISBN: 978-1-300-76771-8

GUN CONTROL THEATRE ACTION

History:

NoPassport theatre alliance and press in collaboration with force/collision, Theater J and Twinbiz NYC commissioned and presented an evening of short works in support of gun control on January 26, 2013 at Georgetown University's Gonda Theatre in Washington D.C. directed by force/collision to coincide with Molly Smith and Suzanne Blue Star Boy's citizen-artist-instigated March on Washington for Gun Control. The DC event was curated by Caridad Svich and Zac Kline (NoPassport dramaturge) with additional curatorial support from force/collision.

A simultaneous event took place on the same day in collaboration with Pittsburgh PACT (along with One Pittsburgh and CeaseFirePA) curated by Kyle Bostian and Tammy Ryan.

The performance works in this collection were, except where noted, written expressly for these events through direct commission or sent in to NoPassport via an open call.

They may be performed as stand-alone pieces or assembled in an order to make an evening of or marathon event of theatre.

SPECIAL THANKS:

Ari Roth, Theatre J staff, Georgetown University, Dr. Derek Goldman, Dept. of Theater and Performance Studies, Toby Clark, Associate Director of Programs, Dept. of Theater and Performance Studies, Dept. of Theater and Performance studies staff, Heather Helinsky, Jocelyn Kuritsky, Molly Smith, Suzanne Blue Star Boy, Tony Adams and all the wonderful authors who contributed pieces to Gun Control Theatre Action, and to the actors and directors who donated their time.

PLEASE CONDISDER:

Please give a listen to another artist's response to the tragedy in Newton, *ABC's in Heaven* by Carla Gordon and Wayne Richard http://www.youtube.com/watch?v=-nLet4FwuWw

DRAMATURGY NOTE:

Artists must react. Artists must react to the world around them to be fully engaged as artists and citizens. They must react to what they see in the world that inspires beauty, and also what troubles them, what makes them questions, what makes them want to effect change and makes them want to seek out a dialogue with others. The artist's responsibility is not to answer questions, but surely to ask them. Today we are asking questions, today we are engaging in that dialogue. Gun control is a serious topic not only in this county, but around the world.

In January 2013, NoPassport Theatre Alliance and Press (Caridad Svich, founder) in collaboration with Theatre J, force/collision and Twinbiz put out a call for new writing about gun control. We received over a hundred submissions from playwrights, poets and theatre-makers of all regard with vibrant and important reactions to the recent events in Newton, Aurora and the continued conversation and debate about guns in America and across the globe.

The pieces you will read today represent just a small fraction of the writing we wish we could share, but also represent a vibrant first step in the conversation. The conversation about gun control must be had. It must be had in our capitols, in our schools, in our town squares, in our churches and mosques and synagogues, and in the lobby of our theatres. We ask you to read the plays in this collection and enjoy, but also ask you to engage with us in this crucial dialogue. Some pieces are calls to action, some are calls to question, some are prayers, but all are part of conversation that we must be having and have too long ignored.

Zac Kline

NoPassport Dramaturge

CHANGE

By Elaine Avila

[Elaine Avila's plays are produced around the world including: Central America (Teatro Lagartija, National Theatre of Panamá); throughout Canada, (Canadian Centre for Theatre Creation, Theatre SKAM); New York City (Ontological-Hysteric Theatre, Hybrid Theatre Works, Occupy the Empty Space); throughout the U.S.; France (upcoming); and London, England (Tracey Neuls, Nordic Nomad). Recent plays: *Jane Austen, Action Figure; Quality: the Shoe Play, La Frontera/The Border.* Selected awards: Victoria Critic's Circle for Best New Play, Canada Council (numerous), Best Production/ Audience Favorite—Festival de Cocos. She has taught in universities from British Columbia to Tasmania, China to Panamá. Publications: NoPassport Press (Jane Austen Action Figure and other Plays, 2012), Canadian Theatre Review, American Theater, Contemporary Theatre Review, Lusitania. She is the former Endowed Chair and Head of the MFA Program in Dramatic Writing at the University of New Mexico, founder of the LEAP Playwriting Program at Vancouver's Arts Club Theater, and currently a Playwrights Theatre Centre Associate. Representation: Playwrights

Guild of Canada, 401 Richmond Street West,
Suite 350 Toronto, Ontario M5V 3A8, Canada/
Telephone: 416-703-0201 Fax: 416-703-0059 E-
mail (General Inquiries): info@
playwrightsguild.ca]

*

"In response to a horrific series of shootings that has sown terror in our communities, victimized tens of thousands of Americans, and left one of its own bleeding and near death in a Tuscon parking lot, Congress has done something quite extraordinary — nothing at all." –Gabrielle Giffords

(Teacher at her desk, grading papers. She stops.)

MARIE: It couldn't happen here
It couldn't
couldn't

(sets down her red pen).

I look around my classroom. Their sweet little bodies. Would I hide them in a closet? This closet? If we escaped out the windows—would it help? Could I lie to a shooter? Would I throw myself—I hope I would--- but ....I'm not trained like a police officer. What if I don't—what if my reflexes--

They're saying my principal should have a
rifle. She 5'4" She's sixty-two years old. She's
stylish. She always wears heels, skirts. I don't
think she's ever held a gun. They're saying I
should carry a gun. I don't see how I could,
mid-lesson, writing on the board—I can't even
find my cell phone. But on the news they say
we should. Carry guns. We should this, we
should that…

The kids asked me 'bout the Wild West. I
encourage them to ask me things. To be
curious.

They said, "everybody carried a gun, but it
was different, right?"
I said, "yeah….they were defending,
protecting… property. And sometimes
…people, from other people. They weren't
…un…hinged." At least I think they weren't.
And then the kids asked what's "unhinged"? I
tried to explain, a person, like a door falling off
its hinges. I swung the door. I showed them a
hinge…. I wanted to get back the lesson but
then-- they asked, "so nowadays all these
unhinged people… they've all got guns, right?
" I changed the subject.
I could tell they wanted to talk, to figure it out,
to help.
But there was this handout the school gave us
teachers after the shooting . The handout said

change the subject -- the kids need to be
reassured. It said tell them this isn't happening
to them, it won't happen to them. Even if you
feel you are lying that is what you should say.
To comfort them. So I did. That's we keep
doing. Changing the subject.   Reassuring each
other. Even if we feel we're lying--

It couldn't happen here
Couldn't
It can.

DAD'S GUNS

By Neil Blackadder

[Neil Blackadder translates drama and prose from German and French, specializing in contemporary theatre. His translations of plays by Lukas Bärfuss, Ewald Palmetshofer, Evelyne de la Chenelière, Thomas Arzt, Rebekka Kricheldorf and others have been produced, published, and presented in staged readings. He has received grants from PEN, the Howard Foundation, and the Goethe-Institut, and residencies at the Banff Centre and Ledig House. Neil teaches theatre at Knox College. www.neilblackadder.com]

*

CHARACTERS

ELLEN   late-30s or 40s

ROBERT   Ellen's younger brother by
a few years

SETTING

A nondescript room in a rural or suburban American house. A table, two or three chairs, some other pieces of furniture.

TIME

The present.

[Author's Note: I have conferred with a lawyer regarding the frequent quoting from songs (not yet in the public domain) by the two characters. While the definition of "fair use" is imprecise and open to interpretation, the lawyer's judgment was that given the small number of lines quoted from any given song, there would almost certainly be no rights issue involved in producing this play.]

(ELLEN sits at the table, which is covered with different kinds of guns. She's cleaning them: with special brushes, she cleans out barrels; she applies oil to mechanisms and wipes them with special cloths. She carries out this work for some time, very focused, and appearing to take pleasure in what she's doing. Enter ROBERT.)

ROBERT: Hey.

ELLEN: Hi.

ROBERT: (With a sigh, he sits down at the table.) Cleaning them, huh?

ELLEN: Like he taught me.

ROBERT: Do they need it?

ELLEN: Not really.

ROBERT: Well you're getting them nice and shiny.

ELLEN: Shooter's Choice. Dad swore by it.

ROBERT: Didn't he buy stocks?

ELLEN: He sure did.

ROBERT: Smart move.

ELLEN: Smart man.

ROBERT: They're not loaded, are they?

(ELLEN looks at him as if that's an absurd question, and carries on with the cleaning. He picks up a rifle, inspects it.)

ROBERT: So heavy. Nice wood.

(He stands up, and tries to hold the gun in shooting position.)

ELLEN: Pull your elbow into your body. And don't hold it so tightly.

(He follows her instructions. Once he feels more comfortable holding it, he practices taking aim at a few places at random.)

ROBERT: What are we going to do with them?
ELLEN: I'll register them in my name.
ROBERT: So you'll keep them all.
ELLEN: Sure.

(ROBERT holds the gun as if it's a guitar.)

ROBERT: (Singing.) And his mother cried as he
    walked out
Don't take your guns to town son
Leave your guns at home Bill
Don't take your guns to town
ELLEN: Me and Dad used to listen to Johnny
    Cash when we were down here.
ROBERT: And did you talk much?
ELLEN: Not really. It was nice.
ROBERT: Huh.

(ROBERT now holds the gun/guitar in a lower-slung position.)

ROBERT: (Singing.)
Hey Joe, where you goin' with that gun in your
hand
I'm goin' down to shoot my ol' lady
I caught her messin' round with another man
ELLEN: Somehow I can't imagine Dad
    listening to Hendrix.
ROBERT: Me either. Of course, I have as much
    right to them as you do.
ELLEN: To the guns?

ROBERT: Well yes. What if I say I want us to
    get rid of them?
ELLEN: Is that what you're saying?
ROBERT: It might be.
ELLEN: So you've had nothing to do with
    them since you were a kid, and I spent
    hours with Dad out hunting, and down
    here, and now you want to stop me
    having them?
ROBERT: Maybe. Or not. I just ... *(Pause. He
looks at the gun again.)*
Remember that time we went to see the
Marines, doing that, what do they call it?
ELLEN: Drill.
ROBERT: Right.
ELLEN: They were great.

*(ROBERT, still holding the rifle, walks further
away from the table and begins trying to execute the
kind of moves used by silent drill teams, first
marching in place, then rhythmically moving the
rifle from one position to another. As he gets better
at it, he starts to march across the stage, tries a
complicated maneuver to turn around, almost drops
the gun, and comes to a stop, standing to attention
with the rifle at his side.)*

ROBERT: They must practice for hours. Like
    with playing an instrument. Maybe I
    should've joined the Marines.
ELLEN: You'd have made Dad proud.

ROBERT: That's for sure. Hard to imagine,
    though.
ELLEN: Right. And think what he'd have said
    if we'd told him you were getting the
    guns.
ROBERT: I guess he was a pretty responsible
    gun-owner.
ELLEN: Of course he was. And I will be too.
ROBERT: Yes, I know.

*(ROBERT puts the rifle back on the table and sits
back down. He picks up a revolver, opens and looks
in the chamber, then spins the chamber as in
Russian roulette, puts the gun to his head,
theatrically looks over at her as if this might be the
last time they see each other, and pulls the trigger.
She pointedly doesn't react.)*

ROBERT: You saw that film, right?
ELLEN: Sure. A long time ago.
ROBERT: Did Dad ever see it?
ELLEN: I doubt it.

*(ROBERT puts the revolver back on the table and
picks up a shotgun with a scope attached.)*

ROBERT: This is what he'd have used for
    hunting deer, right?
ELLEN: (Looking up.) Yeah, depending.

(ROBERT stands up and begins to stalk an invisible deer, looking intently through the scope and trying various different positions as he tracks his target. Then he relaxes, looking disappointed.)

ROBERT: Damn, it got away.
ELLEN: It can happen.
ROBERT: To you?
ELLEN: Sure.
ROBERT: To Dad?
 ELLEN: Even to Dad. It's normal. It's not the
    worst thing that can happen.
ROBERT: So what is?
ELLEN: If you hit a deer but in the wrong spot.
    So you've wounded it but not killed it.
ROBERT: What happens then?
ELLEN: Well you have to kill it. It's the law.
    But stalking and trying to finish off a
    wounded deer, that's no fun.
ROBERT: Huh.

(Pause.)

ROBERT: (Singing.)
I shot the sheriff
But I did not shoot his deputy
No no no
ROBERT and ELLEN: (Singing together.)
I shot the sheriff
But I swear it was in self-defense

(ROBERT *puts the shotgun back on the table and picks up a revolver with a long barrel. He walks to centerstage, and pretends to be fighting in a duel: he stands very straight, facing either stage left or stage right, and holds the gun against his chest. He then solemnly walks several paces forward, turns, holds his arm out straight, pulls the trigger, and makes a shooting sound.*)

ROBERT: Sorry, old chap. But without honor, a man has nothing.

ELLEN: Two guys fought a duel like that a few months back, over on the other side of the interstate.

ROBERT: Really? The whole thing, back-to-back, twelve paces?

ELLEN: That's what I heard. They even had seconds.

ROBERT: Wow. And what happened?

ELLEN: One of them missed completely, and the other one hit him in the shoulder.

ROBERT: That's funny. Kind of.

(*Pause.*)

ROBERT: So, it's all safe here, right, I mean, the guns, nothing's going to happen with them?

ELLEN: Trust me.

ROBERT: OK.

ELLEN: You trusted Dad.

ROBERT: Well yes, but that was different. I didn't have much choice, I guess.
ELLEN: They'll be fine. It'll all be fine.
(Singing.)
And from under her velvet gown,
She drew a gun and shot her lover down,
ROBERT and ELLEN: (Singing together.)
Madam, Miss Otis regrets, she's unable to
       lunch today.
ROBERT: Did Dad like Cole Porter?
ELLEN: He did, but – upstairs, with Mum.
ROBERT: Ah.

(ROBERT *takes a second revolver from the table and walks to the opposite side of the stage from where he walked for the duel. He faces back across the stage and takes up a stance like a cowboy about to take part in a gunfight: he sets himself with his legs slightly apart, then puts the two guns in the pockets of his pants, one on each side, as if in holsters. He whistles the theme to "The Good, the Bad, and the Ugly," pauses, concentrates, then quickly draws both guns and again makes a shooting sound. Theatrically, he blows the smoke away from the barrel of first one gun then the other, and returns them to his pockets. He then stops performing, takes the two guns back out of his pockets, puts them back on the table, and sits down. ELLEN smiles at him. By now she's finished the cleaning process, and she's tidying up the cloths, lubricants, etc.)*

ELLEN: (Singing.)
Happiness is a warm gun
Bang Bang Shoot Shoot
Happiness is a warm gun, momma
Bang Bang Shoot Shoot

(As she's singing that last line, he suddenly grabs a small revolver - a gun he hasn't previously held, perhaps it was lying on a different part of the table, or elsewhere in the room — and quickly rushes behind one of the chairs, crouching behind it as if using it for protection; she stops what she's doing and looks toward him with some concern. Doing what seems to him in keeping with his play-acting, he flicks a switch on the gun then jumps out, facing the opposite side of the stage, and stands with his legs astride and holding the gun in both hands, like a TV cop.)

ROBERT	ELLEN
Freeze!	Watch out!

(He pulls the trigger. The gun, which was loaded, fires.)

ROBERT: Fuck!

(He throws the gun to the floor in horror.)

ROBERT: Jesus Christ!

ELLEN: What the hell?!

ROBERT: (now sitting on the floor, clutching his knees to his chest)

Fuck, fuck!

ELLEN: You took the safety off, why did you take the safety off?

ROBERT: They're not supposed to be loaded, you said they weren't loaded.

ELLEN: Why would you do that?

(She has retrieved the gun from the floor and reset the safety. She inspects the gun as if concerned about its wellbeing, virtually cradling it.)

ELLEN: Jesus.

ROBERT: Fuck.

IRONY OF THE SECOND DEGREE

By Kyle Bostian

[Kyle Bostian is a playwright, dramaturg, director, and producer – specializing in new works – as well as a "recovering" academic. He holds an MFA in Playwriting from the University of Washington and a PhD in Theatre and Dramaturgy from Florida State University, and he served on the faculties of Point Park University and the University of Wisconsin – Stevens Point. His plays have been finalists or semifinalists in national competitions (SETC Getchell Award, Marc A. Klein Award, Siena College, Young Playwrights) and have had readings or productions at university (UW, FSU, UWSP) and professional (Asolo, Stageworks Tampa, Pittsburgh Playhouse, Bricolage, Kelly-Strayhorn) venues. Kyle is also the founder of two independent companies: NEW stAGE and Pittsburgh PACT (Public Action Communitarian Theatre). He's a member of the Dramatists Guild of America and the Playwrights' Center of Minneapolis. For performance rights or other inquiries, contact the author: Kyle Bostian, kbostian67@gmail.com]

*

A flashlight beam sweeps across stage, stopping when it illuminates a WOMAN asleep in a bed. As the operator of the flashlight approaches the bed, the beam shifts to a nearby nightstand.

A gloved hand opens the nightstand drawer. The flashlight operator shines the beam inside. The gloved hand reaches into the drawer and removes a handgun.
The flashlight operator tucks the light under one arm and checks to see if the gun is loaded. The flashlight operator chambers a round.

The flashlight operator turns on a bedside lamp, revealing him to be a MASKED MAN. As he sets the flashlight onto the nightstand, the WOMAN awakens.
When she sees the MASKED MAN, the WOMAN reaches toward the nightstand drawer. He smiles and shows her the gun as he covers her mouth with his other hand.

MASKED MAN: Marlene Fredericks?
The WOMAN shakes her head.
MASKED MAN: You're not Marlene Fredericks?

She shakes her head emphatically.

MASKED MAN: Then who the hell are you?

He cautiously takes his hand away from her mouth.

WOMAN: Tina. I'm Tina Fredericks. Marlene's daughter.

The MASKED MAN paces along the side of the bed, then aims the gun at the WOMAN.

MASKED MAN: Where can I find her? Your mother.
WOMAN: You can't. Not to speak to anyway. I suppose you can find her grave. She beat you to it.
MASKED MAN: No no no! You have got to be -- ... Hang on. Just how long has she been dead?
WOMAN: About a month.
MASKED MAN: About a month?

The WOMAN nods. The MASKED MAN grabs a nearby robe and tosses it to her.

MASKED MAN: Get up!

The WOMAN gets up and puts on the robe.

MASKED MAN: Now get on your knees.

The WOMAN does so. The MASKED MAN aims the gun at her with a trembling hand and then turns his face away.

WOMAN: Hey! Look at me. If you're gonna shoot me in the head, I want it to be a clean kill.

The MASKED MAN steps over and forcefully presses the gun barrel against her forehead. He partially covers his eyes.

WOMAN: Wait! Take off the mask. I wanna see the face of the man who murders me. You owe me that much.

The MASKED MAN contemplates. He steps back, keeping the gun aimed at her. He removes the mask. They stare at each other.
WOMAN: You look familiar.
(UN)MASKED MAN: I bet I do. I bet I look familiar to you, Marlene.
WOMAN: I'm not Marlene. I told you that. She's been dead for --

The (UN)MASKED MAN takes a paper from his pocket and thrusts it at her.

(UN)MASKED MAN: Oh you're not, huh? So tell me. How is it that your mother Marlene –

who's been dead for about a month -- signed this petition two weeks ago?

WOMAN: She didn't. I did. I signed it under her name.

(UN)MASKED MAN: You -- ... Under the name of a dead woman. Your dead mother. Whose address you share. You really think you can worm your way out of this with such a blatant lie?

WOMAN: I have no idea what this is. But I'm not lying. And, yes, it's her house. I moved in after --

(UN)MASKED MAN: That makes no sense! Who signs a petition --

WOMAN: I'll tell you what makes no sense. It makes no sense you broke into a house intending to shoot my mother, with her own gun, apparently because you thought she signed that petition -- a petition you yourself stood in the cold collecting signatures for. And what makes even less sense is it's a petition to uphold gun rights! To uphold them absolutely.

(UN)MASKED MAN: It's fake! The petition is fake.

WOMAN: Yeah. I get that part. Still doesn't make any sense.

(UN)MASKED MAN: About a month ago. A guy went on a shooting spree. At the Galleria.

WOMAN: I remember.

(UN)MASKED MAN: A middle-aged man with a semi-automatic rifle. He killed ten people, including himself. The other nine were innocent victims. Randomly chosen innocent victims. Nine people who died for no reason.

WOMAN: Did you know someone? One of the victims.

(UN)MASKED MAN: No. But I might have! Any one of them could've been someone I knew.

WOMAN: Someone you loved.

(UN)MASKED MAN: Exactly! Or even me! (beat) I didn't have to know them personally to feel it personally. (beat) It looked like maybe their deaths wouldn't be completely pointless. Such an outpouring of civic grief! And outrage. Calls for action. Real action. Maybe this time something good would come from yet another unspeakable -- and avoidable -- tragedy.

WOMAN: But it didn't last.

(UN)MASKED MAN: It never does. As usual, our so-called leaders caved. On behalf of a populace that, our so-called leaders said, had a right to adequately protect themselves in a dangerous world.

WOMAN: My mother always said it's a dangerous world.

(UN)MASKED MAN: So I made that petition. A petition for people who think guns make them safer. People who think we'd all be safer if more people carried around concealed weapons. People who think public access to assault rifles and armor-piercing bullets makes us safer. I wanted to find out who these people were. It makes me sick knowing they're out there.

WOMAN: What would make you feel better? If they were dead? You're going to break into their houses and shoot them all? (beat) Oh, I get it now. With their own guns! Poetic justice.

(UN)MASKED MAN: Not all of them. Nine of them. Selected from that petition at random. Like the shooter's innocent victims. (beat) But unlike those victims, these people deserve to die.

WOMAN: Deserve to die! For wanting to feel safe in a dangerous world?

(UN)MASKED MAN: They're responsible for making the world even more dangerous. There are studies, and statistics. Countries with stricter gun control have far fewer gun deaths. Having a gun in the home dramatically increases the odds of someone living there being shot and killed.

WOMAN: Studies and statistics? Studies and statistics don't change how people feel. Having that gun beside her bed made my mother feel safe. She had a right to feel safe in her own home. Pretty low odds some nut breaks in and uses her gun to kill her because of her beliefs.

(UN)MASKED MAN: And exactly where do you stand on the issue?

WOMAN: Ah. Now we're coming to it. Am I a suitable substitute for my mother?

(UN)MASKED MAN: You did sign the petition. Even if it was in her name.

WOMAN: If my mother had a concealed carry permit she might still be alive. That's what I think. That's why I signed in her name. (beat) Would you like to know how she died?

(UN)MASKED MAN: I just want to know where you stand.

The WOMAN gets up. The (UN)MASKED MAN backs away with the gun raised.

WOMAN: I stand right here. I stand my ground right here. You really got what it takes to shoot me? To shoot anyone? Nine anyones. (beat) Look in the drawer. Where you found her gun.

The (UN)MASKED MAN crosses to the nightstand and peers into the drawer. He lifts out a newspaper clipping.

(UN)MASKED MAN: "Galleria Gunman Kills Nine."

WOMAN: Keep reading. Fourth paragraph. Where they list the names of the victims.

He scans the article for a moment.

(UN)MASKED MAN: Oh, god. (beat) I'm sorry.

WOMAN: Thanks. Me too.

She reaches a hand out toward him. He stares at her.

(UN)MASKED MAN: I'm so angry. And scared.
WOMAN: I understand. It's a dangerous world.

The WOMAN reaches her hand out farther. The (UN)MASKED MAN raises the gun. It's not clear if he's aiming it at her or offering it to her.

END OF PLAY

50 GUNS

By Alex Broun

[Alex Broun. Born in Sydney, Australia, Mr.
Broun has enjoyed considerable success in
theater, TV and film as a writer, actor and
director. He has had many plays performed in
the USA, South Africa, Singapore, the UK,
Taiwan, Malaysia, the Philippines and
Australia. He has also had many short films
made of his work and has been twice funded
by the Australian Film Commission. A
specialist in ten minute plays, in recent years
he has had over 50 short plays in over 250
productions across the globe. He is currently
the Artistic Director of Short + Sweet -- the
largest ten-minute theater festival in the world
-- in Sydney and Brisbane.
www.alexbroun.com]

*

Characters

EMMA

PLAYWRIGHT'S NOTE

The 'guns' can be as realistic, non-realistic or symbolic as the director or designer desires. They can be represented by replicas, toys, blocks of wood or as one recent production in Melbourne, Australia - apples. It is only important that one of the objects used clearly stands out as the red 'gun'.

EMMA ENTERS CARRYING A LARGE BOX. SHE STANDS CENTRE STAGE. PAUSE.

EMMA EMPTIES THE BOX, 50 'GUNS' CLATTER ON TO STAGE. ALL ARE THE SAME COLOUR EXCEPT ONE, WHICH IS RED AND EASILY IDENTIFIABLE. EMMA PICKS UP A 'GUN'.

EMMA: I have always been fascinated by guns. Their sleekness, their shinyness, the elegance of their design.

1. Friday, October 25th, 1415. An unknown English soldier killed by a French soldier at the Battle of Agincourt. The first person ever killed by a gun

SHE PLACES THE 'GUN' IN THE BOX.

Guns know who they are. They do not experience existential doubt. Whatever happens the gun is still a gun.

SHE PICKS UP ANOTHER 'GUN'.

2. 15 July 1974. Christine Chubbuck, committed suicide during a live broadcast. At 9:38 am, 8 minutes into her talk show, on WXLT-TV in Sarasota, Florida, she drew out a revolver and shot herself in the head. Christine had been struggling with depression and suicidal tendencies. Bet the ratings were good that day.

SHE PLACES THE 'GUN' IN THE BOX.

Some say guns are evil. Anything created solely for the purpose of destroying other human beings must be evil.

SHE PICKS UP ANOTHER 'GUN'.

3. 14th of December, 2012, Newtown, Connecticut. Six-year old Dylan Hockley is one of 20 children killed at Sandy Hook Elementary School when twenty-year-old Adam Lanza opens fire on Dylan's class with a military style Bushmaster .223 semiautomatic rifle. All of the children killed are between the ages of six and seven. The gunman's mother,

Nancy Lanza, volunteered at the school. Nancy is later found dead at her family home. Six female teachers at the school are also killed. The incident was the latest in a series of mass shootings in the US over the last several years. In 2007 32 people were gunned down by a student at Virginia Tech university. President Barrack Obama says: "Our hearts are broken today". Wayne LaPierre, chief executive of the National Rifle Association says: "The only way to stop a bad guy with a gun is a good guy with a gun," and blames rap music, films and violent video games.

SHE PLACES THE 'GUN' IN THE BOX. SHE PICKS UP ANOTHER 'GUN'.

4. Sharidyn Svebakk-Bohn. Utoya island, Norway.

On 22nd of July, 2011 Anders Breivik bombed government buildings in Oslo, Norway, killing eight people. He then took a ferry to Utoya where he shot dead 69 students, including 14-year-old Sharidyn, who were attending a camp of the Workers' Youth League on the island. Breivik outlined the reasons for the killings in a manifesto he posted on line. "Islam and cultural Marxism are the enemy", he wrote, "I seek violent annihilation of Eurabia, multiculturalism and the deportation of all Muslims from Europe."

Sharidyn, the youngest victim of the massacre, was born in New Zealand but had lived most of her life in Norway.

Murder is easy. It's a terrible thing to say but murder is easy. The act itself is simple. You point the gun and pull the trigger. Easy. If that doesn't work, you do it again.

That is power and the gun gives you that power.

SHE PLACES THE 'GUN' IN THE BOX. SHE PICKS UP ANOTHER ONE.

5. Veronica Moser-Sullivan.

Midnight, Friday July 20th, 2012. Aurora, Colorado. A gunman in a gas mask and body armor enters a cinema during the midnight premiere of the new "Batman" movie. After hurling a gas canister into the theater he opens fire on moviegoers with an assault rifle, a shotgun and a pistol. He wounds 59 people and kills twelve, including six-year-old Veronica. "She was a very special girl", said Veronica's grandmother, Anne Moser. "She was very intelligent … she was a sweetheart to everybody, and lovable. She knew how to make people happy."

The shooting evoked memories of the 1999 massacre at Columbine High School in Littleton, 17 miles from Aurora, where two students opened fire and killed 12 students and a teacher.

SHE PLACES THE 'GUN' IN THE BOX. SHE PICKS UP ANOTHER ONE.

March 12, 2006. Yusufiyah, Iraq.

Soldiers of the 502nd Infantry Regiment entered 14-year-old Abeer Qassim Hamza's house and ordered Abeer's father ('GUN' IN THE BOX), mother ('GUN' IN THE BOX) and six-year-old sister ('GUN' IN THE BOX) into another room where Pfc. Steven Green summarily shot all in the head, emerging to say, "I just killed them."
Abeer was held down to the floor by another soldier. Green and at least one other soldier then raped Abeer, and then Green shot and killed her. The lower part of Abeer's body, was then set on fire.

SHE PLACES THE 'GUN' IN THE BOX.

Murder is easy.

SHE PICKS UP ANOTHER 'GUN'.

10. Christopher Pitcock, 17, Oakland, California, USA.

Investigators say the shooting was a robbery gone awry. The gun used was a .38 caliber Smith and Wesson revolver.

According to a report the Smith and Wesson .38 is the most popular gun used in violent crime in the USA.

SHE PLACES THE 'GUN' IN THE BOX

Guns also have no conscience. They do not feel remorse or ask for redemption.

SHE PICKS UP ANOTHER 'GUN'.

March 31st, 1993, Brandon Lee, Wilmington, North Carolina on the set of The Crow

Lee was killed after another actor fired a prop gun at him. A 'squib load' was lodged in the barrel of the handgun. When the blank was fired, the bullet shot out and hit Lee in the abdomen, wounding him fatally.

SHE PLACES THE 'GUN' IN THE BOX.

And guns can not undo what they have done. You can't pull the trigger and bring somebody back. No matter how much you might want to, the genie can never go back in the bottle.

Once the bullet leaves - it's never coming back.

SHE COMES ACROSS THE RED 'GUN'. SHE LOOKS AT THE 'GUN'. BEAT.

SHE MOVES AWAY AND PICKS UP ANOTHER 'GUN'.

(QUICKLY) Aaron Vickers - Ruger 9 mm semiautomatic (SHE PLACES THE 'GUN' IN THE BOX)

Jason Abbott - Lorcin Engineering .380 semiautomatic – (SHE PLACES A 'GUN' IN THE BOX),

Billie Jo Ace - Raven Arms .25 semiautomatic (SHE PLACES A 'GUN' IN THE BOX),

Jorge Alcantar - Mossberg 12 gauge shotgun (SHE PLACES A 'GUN' IN THE BOX)

Michael Daniel Alexander - Smith and Wesson 9mm semiautomatic (SHE PLACES A 'GUN' IN THE BOX),

Earl Booker Juniour – Smith and Wesson .357 revolver (SHE PLACES A 'GUN' IN THE BOX),

Maria Ragland Davis, Bryco Arms .380 semiautomatic (SHE PLACES A 'GUN' IN THE BOX),

Sukhwinder Singh Dhaliwal, Davis Industries .380 semiautomatic (SHE PLACES A 'GUN' IN THE BOX),

SHE COMES ACROSS THE RED 'GUN' AGAIN, SHE LOOKS AT IT AGAIN. BEAT.

August 19th, 1994. Trent Lockett, 20, Toledo, Ohio, USA.

SHE MOVES AWAY FROM THE RED 'GUN' AND PICKS UP ANOTHER 'GUN'.

20. Jim Mullins, 64, Rutledge Pike, Tennessee, USA.

Mullins' regular customers at the Discount store knew where he kept his .38-caliber pistol. The killer knew, too. Mullins was killed with a bullet to the head - all for a cash register with just enough bills to make change.

SHE PLACES THE 'GUN' IN THE BOX, PICKS UP ANOTHER ONE.

2nd of March, 1853. Fort Tennett, Texas

Lieutenant Frederick Denman went out to hunt and fish with a brother officer, when by the accidental discharge of a rifle in the hands of his companion he was fatally shot in the knee.

Unlucky.

SHE PLACES THE 'GUN' IN THE BOX AND PICKS UP ANOTHER ONE.

1802, exact date unknown. Outside Sydney, Australia.

Pemulwuy, legendary Australian Aboriginal "rainbow warrior". Shot dead by Henry Hacking. On the orders of Governor King his head was cut off and sent to England.

SHE PLACES THE 'GUN' IN THE BOX AND PICKS UP ANOTHER ONE.

Sitting Bull, December 15, 1890. Shot by Indian Police leading to the Massacre of Wounded Knee.

SHE PLACES THE 'GUN' IN THE BOX AND PICKS UP ANOTHER ONE.

(PACE QUICKENING) 24. Mahmoud Qabha, a 4 year old Palestinian boy, killed at a checkpoint in the West bank when Israeli soldiers opened fire on his family's pickup truck.

SHE PLACES THE 'GUN' IN THE BOX AND PICKS UP ANOTHER ONE.

Ilana Turgeman, she was 15, Ma'a lot, Israel. One of 22 Israeli students killed by three members of the Democratic Front for the Liberation of Palestine in a massacre in a local high school.

SHE PLACES THE 'GUN' IN THE BOX AND PICKS UP ANOTHER ONE.

Donald Coffey, 7-years-old, Texas, USA. May 10, 2009.
Hit in the face by a shotgun blast while sitting on the back seat of his dad's car after a family outing.

The couple who killed him had posted a sign on their land saying: 'Trespassers will be shot. Survivors will be re-shot!! Smile - I will."

SHE PLACES THE 'GUN' IN THE BOX AND
PICKS UP ANOTHER ONE.

27. Quainta Hynman, aged 8, Arouca, Trinidad
and Tobago, shot five times by the gunman on
the upper and lower back. Found dead by his
grandmother lying in a pool of blood

SHE PLACES THE 'GUN' IN THE BOX AND
PICKS UP ANOTHER ONE.

Minneola, Florida, a10-year-old girl, shot in the
back as she was eating breakfast by her 9-year-
old brother. He must have really hated his
sister.

SHE PLACES THE 'GUN' IN THE BOX AND
PICKS UP ANOTHER ONE.

Rhys Jones, 11, shot dead in Liverpool,
England as he enjoys a kick-about.

SHE PLACES THE 'GUN' IN THE BOX AND
PICKS UP ANOTHER ONE.

13-year-old Nathan Bellar of Lakeland, Florida,
watched his father, Troy, 34, gun down his step
mother, Wendy (PLACES THE 'GUN' IN THE
BOX), as she tried to take her sons to their
grandparents.

Nathan ran back through the house and heard his father shoot his younger brothers - Ryan, 8, (PLACES A 'GUN' IN THE BOX), and Zack, 5 months (PLACES A 'GUN' IN THE BOX).

His father then chased Nathan through the cluttered garage and took aim, but tripped on a bicycle before he could get off the fatal shot. As Nathan ran screaming to the safety of a neighbor's house, his father killed himself on the front lawn.

SHE PLACES A 'GUN' IN THE BOX AND ONCE MORE COMES ACROSS THE RED 'GUN'.

William S. "Trent" Lockett was baby-sitting his 11-year-old sister and a 12-year-old neighbor at the time of the shooting, which was reported just after 7 p.m. Monday at Lockett's home.

BEAT. SHE PICKS UP ANOTHER GUN, SUDDENLY FAST AGAIN.

Andy Warhol ('GUN' IN THE BOX)
Gianni Versace ('GUN' IN THE BOX)

Marvin Gaye ('GUN' IN THE BOX)

Tupac Shakur ('GUN' IN THE BOX)

Selena ('GUN' IN THE BOX)

John Lennon ('GUN' IN THE BOX),

Adolf Hitler ('GUN' IN THE BOX)

SHE COMES ACROSS THE RED 'GUN' AGAIN.

Trent, who recently had enlisted in the Air National Guard and was due to leave for boot camp at Lackland Air Force Base in Texas, was showing his prize .22 calibre rapid fire pistol to his kid sister.

(QUICKLY) Robert F Kennedy ('GUN' IN THE BOX),

John F Kennedy ('GUN' IN THE BOX),

Che Guevara ('GUN' IN THE BOX)

Abraham Lincoln ('GUN' IN THE BOX),

Ghandi ('GUN' IN THE BOX),

ONCE MORE SHE IS CONFRONTED BY THE RED 'GUN'.

Lockett practiced competitive shooting, a sport he had pursued since high school, and was familiar with gun safety, friends say.

"My ultimate goal is to go to the London Olympics," he said.

(QUICKLY) Martin Luther King ('GUN' IN THE BOX)

Malcolm X ('GUN' IN THE BOX)

Trayvon Martin ('GUN' IN THE BOX)

The person who was killed by a gun while I'm saying this sentence.

SHE PLACES THE 'GUN' IN THE BOX. NOW ONLY THE RED 'GUN' REMAINS.

Lockett took the magazine out of the pistol and gave the gun to his sister, unaware that a round was left in the chamber.

SHE SLOWLY PICKS UP THE 'GUN'.

His sister Emma pulled the trigger. The bullet entered her older brother's skull approximately two centimeters below his right temple, penetrating both the temporal and frontal lobes.

Trent was pronounced dead on the scene by emergency personnel.

"It was accidental," said a local Detective. "There was no foul play."

"This is a terrible tragedy. One that his sister will have to live with …"

for the rest of my life.

LIGHTS SLOWLY FADE.

EVERYDAY VILLAINY

By Gab Cody

[Gab Cody's plays have been staged at the
Coconut Grove Playhouse in Miami, the
Williamstown Theatre Festival, Quantum
Theatre and NYC's Urban Stages.
Her film works include shorts and
documentaries that have screened at Greetings
From Pittsburgh: Neighborhood Narratives,
the Cleveland International Film Festival, NYC
Horror Film Fest, San Francisco Independent
Film Festival, San Francisco's Disposable Film
Fest, the 11/22 International Comedy Short
Film Festival in Vienna, Austria, and on
WQED-TV. Gab was recently awarded an
MFA by Point Park University. She earned her
BFA at the University of North Carolina School
of the Arts. Gab attended the Sewanee
Writers' Conference as a Tennessee Williams
scholar in playwriting. Her new bilingual
Franco-English play *Fat Beckett*, which
Playscripts published this year (2013), received
a full production in December, 2011 at
Quantum Theater in Pittsburgh and was
named a top ten production of the year by the
Pittsburgh Post-Gazette. This summer Gab
served as lead writer on Bricolage Production
Company's immersive urban adventure
STRATA, an experience designed

collaboratively by a group of conceptual artists, directors and designers. Her feature film "Progression" is in postproduction and scheduled for completion in 2013.]

*

MARY speaks to the audience.

MARY:

Close your eyes.

Take a breath.

Try to remember the first thing you could ever remember.

(Waiting for the audience to do this, giving them time.)

Open your eyes.

Thank you.

I spend a great deal of time creating characters, some of them drawn from the deep well of unreliable memory. Some things we remember even though they never happened. Memories filled with past heroes and past villains.

The simplest way to make a character that you're creating completely unsympathetic and villainous? Mustache? Single-handedly bankrupting a small town through self-serving avarice? No. According to one of the most-renowned screenplay writers of all time: an audience will never forgive the murder of an innocent dog.

Murder.

Innocence.

Dogs.

My mother's second marriage was to my father. I am the only child from that union. He was an intellectual— she preferred intellectuals. He was a big, tall, swarthy Jewish man from a family in Maryland. My mother was a tall, athletic blond Catholic from California.

There was not an extended family; I never met any of my grandparents.

My father did not like animals. He did not like cats, birds, horses, adorable puffy-cheeked hamsters, playful otters, soft bunnies, graceful gazelles, regal lions... innocent dogs. He was simply NOT an animal person.

By the time they moved to Alaska we lived on a veritable farm. We had goats, horses, rabbits, a monkey, a de-skunked skunk, ponies, German shepherds and a long-haired poodle-mutt-mix named Sally.

When I think about my parents I can only remember how much contempt they had for one another. I have no idea what drew them together or why two such smart people were dumb enough to marry someone who— well, their marriage is the reason I am here, so I'll stop there.

One night a fight erupted in our living room. My mother and father screamed. The children, my half brothers and sister and the two foster kids, taking their safe viewing positions. I was three. I remember the intensity of their anger. I remember my father grabbing the family shotgun. We had a shotgun. We lived in Alaska. I remember the tumble of bodies rushing to the back door of the kitchen. The force of my six-foot tall father pushing forward past my shouting mother, past the children. The rabbit cages had been compromised. Maybe it was Sally the dog, maybe it wasn't. Innocent rabbits had been killed. Maybe by Sally, maybe not.

The outer door swings open. The backporch stairs are wooden. Someone constructed them. They were not made by a machine. My father raises the shotgun, I pull at his leg, my mother grabbing at his arm. All of the children shouting, "Don't shoot Sally, dad!" "Don't shoot!"

My father shoots and kills the family dog.

Her innocence uncertain.

It may come as no shock that they divorced within a year.

When I was a child, my mother explained to me that her mother—my grandmother—had been killed in an accident. The details of this car accident were unknown to me. When she spoke of it my mother expressed herself in sentences that did not invite further conversation.

During a spring break from college, I was twenty-one, we were horseback riding: a four-hour trail ride. My mother grew up on horseback, as did I. Her father had been a deputy sheriff in Redwood City. He carried a gun. It was his job.

Western People.

The Law of the Land.

Horses.

As we pulled our horses into their keep and I
hopped down from the saddle I asked my
mother, "Were you there? During the car
accident? When your mother died?"
One hand still on the horn of the saddle, she
bowed her head for a moment, took a breath
and turned to me: a quizzical face.

"What are you talking about?"

"When your mother died in the car accident.
Were you there? Did you see it?"

"Car accident?"

"Yes."

There was a silence.

"There was no car accident. My mother was
murdered. She was shot."

There was a silence.

"Oh."

"I must have told you she died in an accident. And you thought car accident. It wasn't an accident. She was murdered. I found her. "

My mother had been seven when she found her mother shot dead. She refused to come out of her room for months.

The details are sordid and hard to come by. They never arrested anyone. My grandmother was a model in San Francisco. My mother says she was killed by a jilted lover.

When I met my grand uncle, my grandmother's brother, as an adult, he had trouble speaking to me. Finally, over tea in his kitchen he said, "I'm sorry, I don't mean to stare, but you're just like her. You look like her. You speak like her— your gestures."

Past violence.

New violence.

Childhood.

Innocence.

Close your eyes and try not to remember.

Extract from **TESTIMONY**

By Tameka Cage Conley, PhD

[Tameka Cage Conley, PhD, is a professional literary artist who writes poetry, fiction, and plays. She completed the doctoral degree in English at Louisiana State University where she received the Huel Perkins Doctoral Fellowship. She was later awarded the Distinguished Dissertation Award for her manuscript, Painful Discourses: Borders, Regions, and Representations of Female Circumcision from Africa to America. In 2010, she received the August Wilson Center Fellowship in literary arts. Her first play, *Testimony*, was produced at the Center in May 2011. In fall 2011, she received the Advancing the Black Arts Grant for community-based theater. In 2012, she became a Cave Canem Poetry Fellow and was nominated for the Pushcart Prize for poetry as well as the Carol R. Brown Creative Achievement Award. She is completing her first novel and a poetry collection.]

***

(When the lights come up on the scene, two caskets are on stage. They are open. Bird, age twelve, is in one casket. Jay, age thirteen, is in the other. They

slowly rise out of their caskets. Their movements are methodical and burdened by the weight of death, the skins of their faces matte and glossy, appropriate for the dead. Bird wears a navy suit. Jay wears a gray one. Both wear shiny black shoes. They do not look at each other. Each speaks as if he is alone.)

BIRD: People don't know how many different colors your skin can be when it's brown. Mom took me down South, to South Carolina, a place where my great-great grandmother was born, called Gullah. I was on the beach, and the sand was warm at the bottom of my feet, so I looked down to see how my feet looked in the sand, and when I looked up again, I could see a rainbow on my skin between my wrist and my elbow because the sunlight was hitting me right there, and it was warm, like the sand under my feet. A rainbow! On my skin. Had all kinds of colors: turquoise, yellow, purple, gold. I didn't know rainbows could do that til that day.

JAY: Til that day, I didn't know somebody wanted me to die. I was eight years old with Bird, my best friend. We walked to the store to buy some candy. Just us two was in the store, and a cop had passed, and he looked through the door, right at us, and he turned his fingers into a gun and aimed at us, and his eyes looked so mean, and I knew he was pointing at us cause wasn't no one else in the store. We were scared, but we didn't run. Might've looked scared, but we didn't run. After he drove away, I looked at Bird. I said, "Why did that cop just do that?" He shrugged his shoulders, and his long, brown locs trembled like my bad nerves, and said, "Maybe he want us to die, Jay." I said…why?

BIRD: "Why?" I asked my mom, when she said we had to leave the Gullah three days ahead of time. Someone had quit their job at the hospital, and if she worked extra, she'd get double money. But I told her, the Gullah is where I'm supposed to be, not in Pittsburgh. Pittsburgh don't have a beautiful beach or see-through water and I never saw a rainbow on my skin in Pittsburgh. She said don't I miss my friends? I said just Jay, but if he knew how happy I was, he'd want me to be here, too. Maybe if he could come, we could get back to the time when I looked at him and he looked at me, and we was the same, like when you put our names together and get JayBird. Before I left, Jay didn't look right. He looked like he was always going someplace. Could be standing right in front of you, and it's like he wasn't looking at you, like he wasn't even there. I wish we had quadruple money so me and Jay could've moved to South Carolina and stayed on the beach and not in Pittsburgh.

JAY: In Pittsburgh, the part of Pittsburgh where I live, everybody dead. Even if they alive, they eyes wide open, they dead. It's just a matter of time. Like my cousin, Music, who got killed right outside his house. That's how I learned how shiny blood can be, how if you stare down in it, you can see your face. I saw my face in Music's blood, and the blood kept crawling to my feet, and I heard my own voice, like it was talking to me, it said, "Get outta that blood, you stupid lil nigga," but I couldn't move. After I wiped my tears, I said I would never let what got Music get me. But it did. Seem like nothing I could do.

BIRD: Nothing I could do could prepare me to leave the Gullah. When it was time, I felt like I was leaving a beautiful place to head back into ugly. I had to leave something of me, there. I found a pair of scissors, and cut all my hair I had been growing since I was little. I cut it, and I didn't ask nobody, because it was my hair, and when momma said we had to leave, I couldn't do nothing about that, but when it came to my hair, growing out my own head, from my scalp, I decided, well, I can do this. So I went way down the beach, far away from the house where momma's boss let us stay, and I cut each long loc, one by one. I said goodbye to my head full of friends, and I buried them with my hands, deep in the sand, and it was awesome to see the sand on top and around my skin and my long, brown locs. After I buried it, I prayed. I said, 'God, thanks for letting me see this place I love. Please don't let nobody take my hair out the sand,' and I was sad and happy and peaceful, and then, I could leave. When Momma saw my hair all gone, she covered her mouth and looked like she was about to cry because we started growing our hair at the same time, and that made us closer, like she was my big sister and not just momma. When she asked me why I did it, I said, "I had to."

JAY: I had to. To keep from being killed myself, I had to carry a gun, and the gun made me feel scared and powerful. Scared cause if a cop found a gun on me, I knew that would be it for me, that I'd be headed to juvie or worse. But I felt powerful because I knew if any fool ever tried to step to me, I could pull on him and then it'd be my piece he was stepping to, and not just me. Not just flesh.

BIRD: Just flesh. That's how I felt back in Pittsburgh. My body was there, but the rest of me was in South Carolina. I tried to talk to Jay about how I felt, but he rushed me, like he didn't wanna hear. I think he was jealous that my momma took me away from here. So he didn't want to hear nothing about my trip, except my hair. "Where your hair, man?" he said. "Gone," I told him. He said, "Damn, that's messed up. What happened?" My hair is between God and me. So I said, "Nothing." Then he asked me if I wanted to see something. I said what? When he pulled it out, it was shiny, but I didn't see no rainbows.

JAY: I saw a rainbow. When the gun went off by mistake, and Bird fell back, like the wind from a hurricane was pushing him to the ground, I saw a rainbow in front of his face, like a curtain full of color. It was the first time I had ever seen one, and it was the most horrible thing I have ever seen.

BIRD: The most horrible thing I have ever seen was the rainbow around Jay's face when the bullet landed hot in my chest, and I felt my body going back, back, like something from the ground was pulling me down. Jay's mouth was open, like he couldn't believe what he did, and his face was blue from the light from the sun and the rainbow, and I wonder if he saw it, too, before he looked down on me and ran. I wanted to scream, Don't leave, Jay! But the bullet made it hard to talk. I hated to die.

JAY: I hate how it feels to be a murderer. I hate it so bad, I ran, and left Bird by his self. I ran all the way home, to my bedroom, closed the door, and locked it. I was alone. I remembered all our good times, me and Bird, and my heart broke over and over again, and then I felt an evil thing all around me until it became me and a voice said, "Do it," and I felt so awful, like none of me was worth nothing, so I put the gun to my head, said "Forgive me."

BIRD: And he pulled the trigger.

End Scene.

THE NEXT TIME

By Cecilia Copeland

[Cecilia Copeland Full length works include: Light of Night World Premier with IATI Theatre 2014. COURTING and BIOLIFE Semifinalists for The O'Neill Playwrights Conference. 'The Wicked Son', named among the "Top Three Best New Jewish Plays," by the JPP. One Women, winner of the Lennis J. Holm Scholarship. One Acts: Amusement Bomber adapted into a short film with Metro Screen Australia. BILLBOARDS GREATEST HITS Commissioned and Produced by The Performing Arts High School. Other short works have been produced or presented at the Anarchist Theatre Festival of Montreal, Culture Project, CAPSLOCK THEATRE, Sticky, The Disreputables, Le Petite Morgue, 31 Plays in 31 Days, Ensemble Studios Theatre, INTAR Theatre, Cherry Lane Theatre, and Metro Screen Australia. Cecilia is the Founder and Artistic Director of New York Madness and a Member of the League of Professional Theatre Women. Author: Cecilia Copeland, ceciliacopeland@gmail.com]

*

CHARACTERS:
JANE Mother
JACK Shop Owner

SCENE 1: The Next Time

JACK stands casually behind a counter and JANE enters awkwardly. She surveys the many, many, many guns all   around her. She doesn't know where to start.

JANE: I would like to buy a gun... please.
JACK: Sure, we have all of these you see in front of you and I have a few in the back, and I can order some if you have something special in mind.
JANE: Do I need a license?
JACK: You need a license to carry a concealed firearm.
JANE: Oh... does that mean I can't buy one?
JACK: Of course not, go ahead.
JANE: Well then, how would I get it home? I mean would I put it in a bag and if it goes in a bag isn't it concealed?
JACK: Well, I mean, yes, but you're not carrying it for use.
JANE: But it's concealed then... in the bag.
JACK: You're allowed to bring it home.
JANE: Oh...

JACK: Concealed means like… hiding on your person, you know, like under your shirt or something.

JANE: Huh.

JACK: It doesn't apply to this situation.

JANE: Sure.

JACK: Great. So, which one did you want to buy? What are you looking to shoot?

JANE: I don't know what I want to shoot, I just thought I should have a gun. For… protection I guess.

JACK: Everyone should have a gun for protection.

JANE: But what if I don't know how to use it?

JACK: You just point and shoot.

JANE: Are there rules about me keeping a firearm in my house with kids?

JACK: I mean, obviously you should keep them in a safe place.

JANE: My kids?

JACK: The guns. Keep the guns in a safe place.

JANE: Oh. Like… high up on a shelf?

JACK: Somewhere that the kids can't get to them without supervision.

JANE: Is there a law for that?

JACK: No, that's up to your own discretion.

JANE: What about other children?

JACK: What do you mean?

JANE: I mean if other children come over to my house, am I required by law to register myself as a gun owner so that parents of other children know that if they are leaving their children with me in my home that I have guns?

JACK: No, of course not! That would be a huge invasion of privacy.

JANE: But… hm… You know… I'm sorry.

JACK: What for?

JANE: I don't want to buy a gun.

JACK: If you're worried about gun safety I recommend getting a safe and keeping your guns in a safe.

JANE: I'm worried about my children and keeping my children in a safe place. You see my son went over to our neighbors house… and I kept thinking, and I don't know why I thought this, but I just assumed it would be illegal to have guns laying around within the reach of children, but it's not a law is it?

JACK: Why do you ask?

JANE: I just thought there was some law against it. Reckless endangerment or something. You know like… leaving a crack pipe on the coffee table next to a nine year old. I mean… I just assumed it was illegal.

JACK: We advocate responsible gun ownership.

JANE: But there's no law stipulating a gun has to be under lock and key? There's no actual criminal offense for leaving it out and available?

JACK: I don't think you've come to the right place. I'm a responsible shop owner. I keep my guns under lock and key and the guns I have at home are kept under lock and key. Safes as a matter of fact, with a combination.

JANE: My son Chris accidentally shot himself. He was nine.

JACK: I'm really sorry that happened, but I had nothing to do with that.

JANE: The gun that was used... that he used... was purchased here. At your store and I just wanted to make sure that no laws were broken in all steps along the way.

JACK: We can't require people to keep guns in safes. That's up to the government and nobody wants that. It's an invasion of-

JANE: (She is holding back tears.) I do. I want all guns to be kept in safes and I want you to sign this statement that you won't sell a gun to anyone unless they agree to keep it under lock and key or be prosecuted for reckless endangerment.

JANE gets out the document and puts it on the counter.

JACK: I'm not gonna sign that.

JANE: How about this?

She gets out another document and also gets out a pen and puts them on the counter.

JANE: It's a petition to support stronger gun restrictions and registering who own a gun with the government so that I know if I send my child to someone's house that I know they have guns there?
JACK: I... Look, I'm really sorry that happened to you, but there's really nothing I can do about it.
JANE: Yes there is, you can sign this.
JACK: I...
JANE: Or sign this...

(Gives him another petition.)
JANE: Or sign this.

(Gives him another petition.)

JANE: Or you can close your shop and start selling flowers.
JACK: I can't make a living selling flowers.
JANE: But you can make a killing selling guns.
JACK: I didn't do anything wrong. I didn't. I'm not responsible for what happened.
JANE: If it happens again, and you don't sign this, then you will be responsible the next time. There is something you can do. Please sign this.

Jack signs all the petitions.

Lights Down.

HELLO, MY NAME IS JOE:
A Piece In Support of Gun Control

By Amina Henry

[Amina Henry is a playwright / teaching artist based in New York City. She is a graduate of Yale University (BA English) and has an MA in Performance Studies from New York University. Her plays have been produced or developed by: The Oregon Shakespeare Festival, The Towne Street Theatre, Manhattan Theatre Source (estrogenius festival), The Hive Theatre, The Secret Theatre, the cell theatre, Bowery Poetry Club (Sticky series), Love Creek Productions, Shakespeare's Sister Company, The HERO Theatre, The Brick and Drama of Works. She is currently an MFA Playwriting candidate at Brooklyn College. She is also a 2012-2013 Core Apprentice playwright at The Playwrights Center in Minneapolis. For information on her upcoming projects, go to http://www.aminahenry.wordpress.com/.]

*

1.
Bang. Bang Bang.
Hello, my name is Joe.
You can't know what I go through
Or what I think,

What I feel,
Day after day.
We are strangers but let me tell you.
I was a little boy once whose parents loved
him, whose teachers loved him, whose friends
liked him well enough.
When I had friends.
I have lived in the same city my whole life,
A city with businesses
And houses
And schools
And families
And a low crime rate
And guns.
My father and I were warriors, we wore the
blood of deer, and I have never been afraid
even though sometimes I have felt other thing,
lots of other things.
Bang. Bang Bang.
Listen to my native cry.
I am not afraid.

2.
Bang. Bang Bang.
Hello.
My name is Joe.
We're in a revolution. Here. Now.
The vultures are circling. Look out for the
vultures. Look at my arms, pecked by vultures.
Look at my arms.
In this city that I've always lived in,

In this country that I've always lived in,
In this place of deep deep shameful things
Hidden underneath words
Hidden underneath the earth
Where we can try to forget the disgusting dried
blood smell of disgusting secrets.
But I'm an American.
I'm a fucking American, a Native fucking
American, not an Indian, a native with war
paint on for the war on – the war on –
revolution. The war on terror. Do you know
what I mean? There's terror and we are at war.
Are you a fucking American?
I am not ashamed of who I am.
I am not ashamed of. Who I am.

3.
Bang. Bang Bang.
So, my name is Joe and
Every morning I go to work
The other day I picked up a new gun from the
Walmart because I have a right to do so, I have
a right to bullets, I have a right to every bullet.
Sometimes I get angry. Sometimes I'm so
upset. Because of – all this shit.
But I'm a good person, you know?
I'm just a regular person
and I pay taxes
and I work
and I go to Church every Sunday where I sing
as loud as my voice can stand it.

As loud as anyone can stand it.
I am good even though my arms are covered in
the blood of the past,
even though I eat too much
and buy too much
and take too many drugs sometimes
and drink too many beers sometimes
and watch too much internet porn sometimes
and I get so very angry when I drive my car on
the highway and some fucking
asshole cuts me off, or I have to wait in line,
any line, and the movie I paid good money for
sucks, and my family suggests that I'm not
good enough
because I don't have enough.

4.
Bang. Bang Bang.
My name is Joe.
The vultures are circling. Good thing I have
arms. Look at my arms. These fucking people –
but I'm not afraid, you know? I'm angry, but
I'm not afraid.
Fuck 911.
Fuck the police.
Fuck the government.
Fuck this country.
But I love this country. And fuck the people
who don't belong here. I belong here, right
here, I was raised on Wonder Bread and Kraft

singles, I was raised on television where any
average Joe – my name is Joe – can be a star.
I am a star and I need protection even though
I'm not afraid,
Understand that,
I'm not afraid.
Who's going to protect me? Against all the shit
that could go down?
I'm not afraid even though the world is a scary
place. Someone could get you in your sleep,
pluck your eyes out, fuck you in the ass, make
you cry, steal your car, steal your jewelry, steal
your money, steal your things, leave you for
dead and that person could be someone you
know, someone you see every day in your
neighborhood, some neighbor or even
someone who looks like family.
But I'm not afraid.
I'm not afraid.

5.
Bang. Bang Bang.
I am Joe
And I have so much love inside
And so much hate inside
And so much human stuff,
So many memories
inside
And when I fire my gun it's like the glorious
song of a pressure cooker when
Everything is cooked and ready.

You want to fuck with me? I dare you to fuck with me. Because I'm not afraid. I don't need an army to be a soldier. I don't need a horse to be a cowboy. I don't need a gun to be a man, but I want a gun,

And I have a gun,

And I'll shoot my gun

Because it's my right

Because I'm an American.

The other day I was wondering what it would feel like

To shoot through flesh

Like in the movies

Like on that television show

Like in that video game

Like in that song that I love so much I've played it a thousand times.

I was wondering and I was angry

Because I'm a good guy and there are so many bad guys,

Bad guys who'll try to make a guy like me feel like

He doesn't matter.

And these bad guys are tricksters because they can look like

Your wife

Or your girlfriend

Or your mother

Or your friend

Or your boss

Or some guy wearing the wrong colors on the
wrong side of the street
Or little school children on their way to class
Who maybe one time said something not so
nice
And people should always be nice.
Are you listening to me?

6.
Bang. Bang Bang.
I'm Joe
And I could kill something
or someone for looking at me the wrong way
on the wrong day
at the wrong time
because I just want to shoot
and feel that power surging through me,
that gun power
that American power
that manpower
that angry power
that human power
to fuck shit up,
and did you know that most people are shot by
people that they know,
just like most rapes occur between people who
know each other
and random acts of violence
are generally not random at all
in the random sense
because there is usually a definite aim

or reason
or pattern like the kind I've never seen
in a snowflake because
I don't have those kind of eyes.
Look at my eyes.
Look at me. Look at Joe.
Bang. Bang Bang.
Joe is not afraid.
Joe is an American and Joe thinks
it's gonna be a beautiful day.
It better be a beautiful day or
Bang
Bang
bang

BRIDGE TO BARAKA:
THE PEN INSTEAD OF THE GUN
An Excerpted Adaptation from the One-
Woman Show, *Bridge to Baraka*

By Yvette Heyliger

[Yvette Heyliger is an award-winning
playwright, a director, and a producing
artist/partner in her own company, Twinbiz.
Bridge to Baraka is her first one-woman show
and marks a return to performing since
appearing as "Aunt Sarah" on Cosby Show.
Her play *White House Wives: Operation
Lysistrata!*, was published by
www.indietheaternow.com. She won the 2010
AUDELCO Recognition Award for Excellence
in Black Theatre's August Wilson Playwright
Award for her play, What Would Jesus Do?
Yvette received the NAACP Theatre Award's
"Best Playwright," nomination for her
published play, *Autobiography of A Homegirl.*
Selections are published in Smith and Kraus'
The Best Women's Stage Monologues 2003 and
The Best Stage Scenes 2003. Look for her new
book, What A Piece of Work Is Man!: Full-
Length Plays for Leading Women. Yvette
served as an Organizing Fellow for President
Obama's re-election campaign. Yvette is a
member of Moms Demand Action for Gun
Sense in America (formerly One Million Moms

for Gun Control) and a proud member of the
Dramatists Guild.]

*

YVETTE X:

Calling black people
Calling all black people, man woman child
Wherever you are, calling you, urgent, come in
Black People...
come
 on in.

That was an excerpt of a poem called, "SOS,"
written by poet, activist, and creator of the
Black Arts movement, Amiri Baraka. The
Black Arts Movement began in response to the
declaration of war that was the assassination of
El-Hajj Malik El-Shabazz, better known as
Brother Malcolm X.

Is there anybody here that was around in the
60's? Well, there's a lot more to it than what
you might remember—more to it than a bunch
of angry poems, rioting and finger pointing.
The pioneers of the modern gun rights
movement emerged during that time. Can you
guess who they were? Anybody? No?

Well, hold on to your seats. This is going to shock you. The pioneers of the modern gun rights movement were... the Black Panther Party for Self-Defense, better known as the Black Panthers. I know; surprised me too. See in the mid-1960's Black folks had won the right to vote, to sit at white lunch counters, in the front of the bus or next to white children in class, but the day-to-day life for most black folks was still the same — poverty, unemployment, lack of education and health care. Only the wealthiest could legally afford guns. America had decided we were citizens, but were slow to deliver equal opportunity for blacks — and, to add injury to insult, blacks were subjected to un-checked violence at the hands of those whose jobs it was to protect and serve them — the police.

(Chanting.) "Arm yourself or harm yourself! Arm yourself or harm yourself! Arm yourself or harm yourself!" No longer content to turn the other cheek or wait until they get to the gold paved streets of heaven to get their milk and honey, you had a whole lot of fed-up, angry Black folks wanting to take some white folks out!

But dig this. Because of Amiri Baraka's Black Arts Movement, some blacks folks chose the pen INSTEAD of the gun as a means of armed self-defense against the System—not caring what "The Man" thought about it, or if he would ever read it, review it, or buy a ticket to see it—"Whitey did this to us." "Whitey did that to us." White folks don't know how close they came—just and ellipsis, an em dash, or a comma away from meetin' their maker! American had never seen such a militant literary movement.

But some blacks weren't content with turning poetry into bullets. Under the Second Amendment, Malcolm told us, it was our right to bear arms. Because the United States government was "either unable or unwilling to protect the lives and property" of blacks, we had to defend themselves "by any means necessary." Huey Newton co-founder, along with Bobby Seal, of the Black Panther Party for Self-Defense, agreed. He hatched a plan to send a message to law makers about the Black Panther Party's opposition to any new gun control legislation.

May 2, 1967. The California Statehouse; home of the offices of the shiny new Governor, Ronald Reagan, and Republican Assemblyman Don Mulford who wanted to disarm the six-month-old Black Panther Party. Twenty-four hand-picked, beret-wearing, uniform-clad Black Panthers climbed the sunny state capitol steps carrying .357 Magnums, 12-gauge shotguns, and .45-caliber pistols in full view of the public. It's hard to believe but, California law allowed its citizens to carry guns at the time, so long as they were visible and not pointed at anyone.

Bobby Seal, read from a prepared statement:

"The American people in general and the black people in particular must take careful note of the racist California legislature aimed at keeping the black people disarmed and powerless. Black people have begged, prayed, petitioned, demonstrated and everything else to get the racist power structure of America to right the wrongs which have historically been perpetuated against black people. The time has come for black people to arm themselves against this terror before it is too late."

Then you know what those Black Panthers did? They waltzed right into the Statehouse, loaded guns and all... and the modern-gun rights movement was born!

Well, there was no problem getting California Republicans to support gun control after that! Couldn't do it fast enough! Governor Reagan told reporters that he saw, "no reason why, on the street today, a citizen should be carrying loaded weapons." He called guns a "ridiculous way to solve problems that have to be solved among people of good will," and "he didn't know of any sportsman who leaves his home carrying a loaded gun." The Mulford Act, he said, "would work no hardship on the honest citizen." And that is how the state of California came to have the strictest gun control laws in the nation at that time.

Now, let's be real. Early gun control laws in this great country of ours were out-and-out racist and elitist. You can believe the NRA, the KKK and GOP were all for gun control when it came to black folks and the poor! But, what's good for the goose is good for the gander. White conservative, God-fearing rural or small town American citizens were affected by these laws too, and therein lies the rub.

Newtown, Columbine, Virginia Tech, Waco and Webster; Hadiya Pendleton, Ramarley Graham, Gabby Gifford, Trayvon Martin, Sean Bell, Amadou Diallo, Malcom X, Martin Luther King, Bobby Kennedy, Jack Kennedy and the all the people who are going to be shot in America today COMBINED, are not going to get Congress to move on this. We have to do it.
Shoot—I bet if you put some beret-wearing' black and brown folks totin' some military-

style assault weapons on the steps of the Capitol, you'll see how fast gun regulation gets passed! Hey—there's an idea...

My name is Yvette X, and if you want to ensure that not another child—black or white; red, yellow, purple or green, gets killed tomorrow; or the day after that; or the day after that, then... *Calling you. Calling all you every-day American citizens; wherever you are. Urgent. Meet me on the steps of the Capitol you law-abiding, church-goin', background-check-passin', paid-your-fair-share-of-taxes-and-then-some, duck-huntin' Constitutional-right-to-bear-arms-if-you-want-to (or not!), citizens... meet me on the Capitol steps!*

THE END

<u>WHAT ARE WE GOING TO DO ABOUT LITTLE BROTHER?</u>

A Play for Two or More Actors

By Zac Kline

[Zac Kline is a nationally produced playwright, bookwriter/lyricist and dramaturge. His play *Big Star California* a one-person show developed with and performed by Blair Baker received a sold-out production in the Philadelphia Live-Arts and Fringe Festival. His play *Messed Up Here Tonight* was featured as the cover story of <u>Our Town</u> the newspaper of the East Side of Manhattan and completed a sold-out site-specific run. Other work has been produced and developed by: Prospect Theater Company, NY International Fringe Festival, Figment Festival on Governor's Island, The University of Oklahoma City, Emerging Artists Theatre and The New Group/24 Hour Play Company. He is the co-founder of Missing Bolts Productions, a small production group devoted to new plays and innovative music theatre. BFA/MFA Tisch at NYU. Thanks to Caridad, the *Spark* team and Blair (always). www.missingbolts.com]

*

Teacher found a note. Teacher found a note that she said said some mean and nasty and scary things. Teacher found note that she said some mean and nasty and scary things and she said that she doesn't want us to be alarmed, but that we should be alarmed. Teacher said she found a note that said some mean and nasty, sad, scary, alarming things. Teacher said she found a note written by little brother.

What are we going to do about little brother? We're going to ask him if he wrote the note. We're going to tell him that the note was wrong.

We're going to ask him if he's really feeling these things, and if he is, why he's feeling them.

We're going to tell him that him that the note was unacceptable.

We're going to tell him that we love him.

We're going to tell him that these thoughts are unacceptable.

We're going to tell him that we love him just the same, that we're always going to love him. We're going to tell him these thoughts have to stop now.

We're going to help him, that's what we're going to do for little brother.

We're going to tell them that these feelings are going to stop. That's what we're going to do about little brother.

Little boys run around the schoolyard pretending that their tiny hands are guns. They run, point, fire, BANG, fall down, die, get up and do it over-and-over again.

I drove little brother to school today, and he told me he didn't want to go in, then he shrugged it off, shrugged it off and said he was okay.

I ask him if he's really okay, and he says: yes, fine.

It's Friday afternoon and little brother is in the car coming from school, he's in the car and I ask him what he's doing tonight, and he says nothing. I ask him if he wants to order a pizza and have a friend over. He says nothing.

I asked him about his friend Jason ... His friend Andy ... Fred ... Billy ... he says he doesn't have any friends.

There was one, their used to be video games, their used to be long afternoons in the basement. He says no, he doesn't have any friends.

Little boys run around the schoolyard pretending that their tiny hands are guns. They pretend in Colorado, they pretend in New York.

Little brother comes home from school one day, he's frazzled, he's bloody. Little brother doesn't want to talk about what happened, he says that NOTHING has happened.

Little brother does well in school.

I need to clean the dried blood from under your nose, I need to wash the violence off your face.

Little brother does very well in school.

He goes to school the next day, he's afraid not to.

I go to the school the next day, they say nothing, they say they don't know anything about what happened.

Little brother is going to go to college.

Little brother gets sadder, and sadder and sadder and doesn't say a word.

He's going to become a doctor.

I drive him to the therapist, but I don't have insurance.

I drive him to the therapist, but we don't have a therapist in our town.

I drive him to the therapist, but my mother, my father, my sister, my brother, my friends, my town says no. He's fine, say he'll grow out of it, leave well enough alone.

He's going to make us proud, he's going to be different than the rest of us.

So I leave well enough alone.

They pretend in Connecticut, they pretend in Virginia.

Little brother goes to school, because he doesn't know what else to do. What do you do when a child hates school, when your child hates school … You make him go, you make him go to school.

They pretend in Texas they pretend in Louisiana.

I tell him to go, I tell him that he doesn't look sick, that he doesn't feel sick, I tell him how to feel, to feel okay to act okay to act like everyone else.
He tries. He tries his best, which becomes his worst. He tries and it hurts.
He doesn't come home bloody ever again, at least not with blood that I can see.
But he comes home each day with different eyes. Harder and harder, cold-and- colder.
When he was a little boy they used to build castles, they used to tell stories, **they** used to do math. But now ... They just stare.
You're doing all right though, you're doing fine.
You're invisible, but you don't want to be invisible.
They pretend in London, they pretend in Paris, they pretend in Doho, they pretend in every spot across the whole wide world.
You're invisible and there's screaming inside your head.
You're invisible, and when they see you, they laugh at you, when they laugh at you all the time, you don't want to be invisible anymore.
We see it, we see it all.
You're asking for help little brother. But we say, no, we saw no.

Teacher found a note. She found a note, he
found a note, we found a note:
Je suis dans la douleur.
Ich habe Schmerzen.
الأ م ف ي أن ا
我很痛苦
לי כואב
Estoy en el dolor.
I am in pain.
In every language, every single language
under the sun.
Please help me, I am in pain. Please help me,
before my hurt, means me hurting others.
Before hurting the whole world again.

Over-and-over again.
Please.
Over-and-over again.
Please.
Over-and-over again.
Please.
Over-and-over again.

CECILY

By Neil LaBute

[Neil LaBute is a writer/circtor. Theatre
includes: *Bash: Latter-Day Plays* (Douglas
Fairbanks Theatre, Almeida Theatre); *The Shape
of Things* (Almeida Theatre, Promenade
Theatre); *The Distance from Here* (MCC Theatre,
Almeida Theatre); *The Mercy Seat* (MCC
Theatre, Almeida Theatre); *Filthy Talk for
Troubled Times* (MCC Theatre); *Fat Pig* (MCC
Theatre, Trafalgar Studios); *Autobahn* (MCC
Theatre); *Some Girl(s)* (Gielgud Theatre, MCC
Theatre); *This is How it Goes* (Donmar
Warehouse, The Public Theatre); Land of the
Dead/Helter Skelter (Ensemble Studio Theatre,
The Bush Theatre); *Wrecks* (Everyman Palace
Theatre, The Public Theatre, The Bush
Theatre); *Woyzeck* (Schauspielhaus Zurich);
Film includes: In the Company of Men; Your
Friends & Neighbors; Nurse Betty; Possession;
The Shape of Things; The Wicker Man;
Lakeview Terrace; Death at a Funeral; Some
Girl(s); Some Velvet Morning; Tumble (short);
After-School Special (short); Sexting (short);
Denise (short); Double or Nothing (short);
Bench Seat (short); Sweet Nothings (short); BFF
(short). Television includes: Bash: Latter-Day
Plays (Showtime). Fiction includes: *Seconds of
Pleasure* (Faber & Faber). He is represented by

Joyce Ketay at the Gersh Agency in New York City. www.gershagency.com.]

*

SILENCE. DARKNESS.

A MAN CROSSES TOWARD US—HE
CARRIES A CRUMPLED BAG FROM
MCDONALD'S UNDER ONE ARM. HE
SMILES.

MAN: ...excuse me? Yeah, hey, sorry. Hi. How
ya doing? You good? Cool. That's great. I was,
ummm, can I ask you something, I mean, like,
quick? Would that be alright? Thanks.
(REACHES IN HIS POCKET) ...I got this sort
of an address here from my wife. (READS) 221
E. Avenue A. #3. See, that's been throwing me
off a bit...I was walking around for a while
once I got down this far and I'm, like...what
the hell? Avenue 'A?' Kind of a name is that?
I'm never gonna find it! That's why I came
over and asked because, that's the way I was
raised. (BEAT) She left me, my wife did.
Cecily's her name, that's her given name,
Cecily, which is kinda beautiful, I guess, but I
always just call her CeeCee, which makes her
smile—it used to, anyway—and I like it.
CeeCee. That doesn't really matter to you,
though, I suppose, but I just thought I'd give

you a little background on us.
Some…whatever you call it…context? Yeah,
that's it. Context. The 'context' is, she took
off on me—left me after ten years of marriage
and two kids at home. She moved away and
wrote me a letter about three weeks ago, said
she hated me—you believe that? Used that
very word, 'hate'—and she says she is never
coming back, don't bother looking for her or
contacting her or any-thing. 'She's done too
much for people in her life and has bottled up
her passions' or some nonsense like that—God,
women come up with some crazy stuff when
they're angry or sad, don't they? I
mean…'passions!' Please. And that she misses
the children but she can't go on 'living a lie'
or something stupid; apparently she's met a
woman and is in love. I got it here, with me--
not that you'd wanna read it-- but I'm carrying
it with me. (HE PRODUCES IT FROM HIS
POCKET, THEN PUTS IT BACK) Point being,
she left me…CeeCee did. I was at work one
day…the kids're off at school…she packed it in
and took off for here. New York City. (BEAT)
Not that I ever would've known that, mind
you, where she went or anything, but that
letter I mentioned…the one I just showed
you…not only does it have the postmark on it
but she writes her damn address up in the
corner, like she was taught to do from the first
day of kindergarten on! How about that one?!

Jesus, she makes me laugh sometimes…like, how ordinary she is, for some-body who really considers herself something special… (BEAT) That note was the first contact we've had, CeeCee and me, since she took off, like, six months ago. (STOPS FOR A MOMENT, GLANCES AT A PAPER BAG HE IS CARRYING) I see you got your eyes on my fast food bag   here, probably wondering just what the hell I'm going on and on about… (WHISPERS) Actually, I got a gun in here. (GRINS) Yep. My old man's .357 Magnum, a real beauty from the 60's. He left it to me when he died. Some kind of cancer took him a few years back and he left me this, a few thousand bucks and one of his cars—my sister got his Buick, though, which sucked. (BEAT) Anyhow, I got that letter--the one from CeeCee--telling me she's found a new life for herself, that she escaped and has now 'liberated' herself from the slavery of, of, of marriage and some other bullshit! So I took a few days off from work, left the kids with my sister and took the   bus out here. Jumped on a Greyhound and, well, hey, you know the rest… and I've been enjoying myself just fine. Seeing the sights and taking my time…walking around. And in a minute or two…once I get my bearings down here… (LOOKS AROUND) I will find that address--this 'A' Street or wherever the hell she's living now, ol' CeeCee--I'm gonna find it and I'm gonna go knock on her door--knock-knock-knock--and when she opens it… I am gonna walk up to her and I'm gonna put the barrel of this revolver right up against her skull…I am. I am gonna do that and then I'm gonna smile at her, smile and lean in real close, all up in her face and I'll whisper, "Was it worth it, CeeCee? 'Finding yourself' like that? I'm curious, sweetie, I really am. I wanna know if it was worth it to you…" (BEAT) Right before I blow her fucking head off.

THE MAN WAITS A BEAT, THEN MOVES TO EXIT. TURNS BACK.

MAN (cont'd): You have a nice day…

HE SMILES AND DISAPPEARS FROM SIGHT.

SILENCE. DARKNESS.

RAND

By Jennifer Maisel

[Jennifer Maisel's *The Last Seder* recently premiered Off-Broadway after productions in Chicago, D.C. and Los Angeles. Plays include *Goody Fucking Two Shoes* (ATL's Humana Festival), *birds* (Rorschach Theatre), *Eden* (Theatre of NOTE) *There or Here* (PlayPenn, NYC's Hypothetical Theatre) . Awards: Kennedy Center's Fund for New American Plays Award, Charlotte Woolard and Roger L. Stevens awards; SCR's California Playwrights Competition; two time PEN West Literary Award finalist; five time Heideman Award finalist. Her *#Sandy* is currently running in Moving Arts' The Car Plays at the Segestrom Performing Arts Center and her *...and the Two Romeos* will be part of E.S.T. - LA Project's Winterfest. She received an Ensemble Studio Theatre/Alfred P. Sloan foundation commission for *Out of Orbit*, developed at the 2010 Sundance Theatre Lab. Her most recent play, Match, was workshopped at the Inaugural University of the Arts Playwrights Festival and the Great Plains Theatre Conference. She also writes for film and television. AGENT: Susan Schulman at Schulman@aol.com]

*

We think someone is setting off firecrackers.

Fireworks, I joke.

Look, after all these years, you still ---

And we are glorying in an evening when the
sun sets late and the house stays quiet

This hasn't happened in recent memory

And this hasn't happened either

Maybe it's that – you keep the cookies around
you so you know you can have them any time
thing and you're not as into eating them any
more

Maybe it's that she's always tired – and yes,
I'm always tired too.

Maybe it's that we've forgotten what feels
good

But right now we are forgetting the forgetting

Because we have a quiet house

The TVs are miraculously off

There's no music drifting from slammed doors

There's no voices, no interruptions, no – no nothing

And I will make you forget about the next email for the next twenty minutes or so

And I will realize I've forgotten your warm hands that I am rediscovering in a way that makes me past and present, the old of the mattress on the floor and the now of king bed the dog likes to burrow under

And all I am hearing is you being loud in a way you haven't been allowed to be loud

But the firecrackers are louder

crack

And I joke about the rekindling of our sex life setting off fourth of july early and then I wish I hadn't spoken because

I see your face

Something passes over your face

And I'm pissed for a moment

Distracted again

I can't even get twenty minutes

And here we go
There you go

To check

For a text, for an email,

You dial them and I am thinking

They are just down block

They are just with their friends

You have to stop this

This worrying, this checking, this hovering

You have to let them

grow up

And I blame you for wrecking the

Rare empty silence of the house

I will never enjoy again.

ELECTRIC MIDNIGHT EMERGENCY CALL

By Lynn Manning

[Lynn Manning is Co-founder and Artistic
Director of Watts Village Theater Company,
dedicated to the development and production
of new theater works that reflect the rich
history and cultural diversity of the
underserved populations of Watts and South
Los Angeles.
www.wattsvillagetheatercompany.org.
Blinded by gun violence at age 23, Lynn has
since built a career as a poet, playwright, actor,
and activist for inclusion of people with
disabilities in the entertainment industry.
www.lynnmanning.com

*

Time tramps
Wide-eyed and slack jawed
Toward electric midnight;
Having peeped the fraud of 'New Age'
mysticism,
I have come full circle
And dance among purple pyramids
To the chamber music of suburban bathroom
chemist;
I am para-sailing the synapses—

On an electro/chemical cruise through tall
cotton;
I am
OUT THERE.

The phone rings;
Its cord,
A pulsing axon to the 'real world;'
Its receiver,
A volatile neural transmitter,
A plastic explosive awaiting my touch.
I gingerly lift it from its cradle.
The ear piece shatters
Flooding my apartment with the sounds and
scents
Of my mother's drunken poverty;
Her desperation looms huge and horrible
Just beyond the grasp of my rational mind;
I have to reel in the ectoplasmic filaments
Extending from my fingertipss;
Command Miles Davis and Herbie Hancock
To cease stirring their foul smelling Bitches
Brew,
And allow this six foot thick shag carpet
Time to retract to its original height.

I say,
        "O.K. Moms. I turned the music down.
        What was that you said?
        You shot the mothahfuckah? What
mothahfuckah?"

The room expands and contracts—
In rhythm with the controlled heaving of my
chest;
The apartment walls become my exoskeleton,
Provide me the volume to contain
The images pouring from this shattered
earpiece:
Some where in South Central Los Angeles,
Just a loogies phlegmatic flight from skid row,
My mother stands,
A smoking gun in one hand
And my throbbing ear in the other;
Her old man lies tossed and twisted on the
filthy floor,
Dying of bullet wounds
And being far too loud about it;
He's oozing
Ancient, alcohol saturated, indigenous
American blood
All over their worm rotted floorboards.

I think,
        Can't the septuagenarian mothahfuckah
stop bitchin'
        Long enough to die quietly?
        I didn't make all that noise when I got
shot;
        when I lay oozing
precious African American Irish Mexican
hemoglobin

into the beer stained carpet of that Vine
Street bar,
my sight sucked down the black hole of
a .32 automatic.

Mom shouts,
"Damn it, bastard! Shut the fuck up!
Ahm tryin' to get yo' ass some help."
I ask,
"Did you call an ambulance? Did you
call the police?"
Mom says,
"Yeah, but I can't get through.
All the lines are busy. That's why I
called you.
may be you can get through up there in
Hollywood.
Get them to send somebody down here
before this old bastard dies on me."

The colors in my apartment
Shift to red hot awareness
Of L.A.'s socio-economic inequities:
Those who most need help can't get it when
they want it.
The South Central Saturday night shootout
Is well under way
And plenty of blood will be oozing
From newly torn button holes
Before dawn shines its search light on the
carnage.

I light a cigarette
And inhale the entire contents of my room;
Frustration pours from my pores
As rationality takes residence.
I say,
        "Just stay cool, Moms.
        I'll call the paramedics as soon as I hang
up.
        Leave the gun in the open and stay
away from it.
        Call me back if you don't hear from
somebody soon.
        If they do show up,
        Call me from the jailhouse when you get
a chance."

The Hollywood emergency operator asks
questions
That test my tenuous cool:
        "Who are you and what's your
involvement?"
        "Why didn't she call on her own?"
        "Why didn't she call from down
there?"
Through rapidly growing teeth and hair
I hip him to the ramifications
Of tax based emergency service,
Check book police protection,
Bid him long life in Primrose Lane,
And hang up.

The rescue now in motion,
I return to slow motion.
I remove a schlitz stalagmite from my
cavernous fridge;
Start that Bitches Brew to boiling again;
Climb back up into the bell of Miles' horn,
And am myself
Blown away.

GUN PLAY

by Oliver Mayer

[Oliver Mayer is the author of over twenty plays, including his two newest plays: FORTUNE IS A WOMAN, about the life and work of Machiavelli, and MEMBERS ONLY, the sequel to his groundbreaking play BLADE TO THE HEAT. His play DARK MATTERS premieres in Spanish as MATERIAS OSCURAS in Colombia this spring. Other plays include WALLOWA: THE VANISHING OF MAUDE LERAY and THE WIGGLE ROOM, as well as DIAS Y FLORES, LAWS OF SYMPATHY, and YOUNG VALIANT. "The Hurt Business: a Critical Portfolio of the Early Works of Oliver Mayer, Plus," is published by Hyperbole Books; "Oliver Mayer: Collected Plays" and "Dark Matters and Other Plays" are published by NoPassport Press. He wrote the libretto for the opera AMERICA TROPICAL, composed by David Conte. Oliver is Associate Professor of Dramatic Writing at the USC School of Theatre. He is the winner of a USC Zumberge Individual Award, and a USC Mellon Mentoring Award for Excellence in Faculty Mentoring of Undergraduates. His literary archive can be found at the Stanford University Libraries Special Collections.

All queries should be addressed to the author:
omayer@usc.edu]
*

A YOUNG WOMAN examines a gun.
A YOUNG MAN IN A HAT watches her,
addresses us.

YOUNG MAN:
How does one negotiate with a gun?
Can it even be done?
Does a good man outdraw a bad one?

(The YOUNG WOMAN opens the gun)

What does one say to a gun?
Does the bullet answer?

(she closes it)

Does the trigger or the finger speak?

(she aims it)

Once it's spoken can we make it stop?

YOUNG WOMAN:
Gun control is an index finger.

(points it at the YOUNG MAN)

YOUNG MAN:
(raises his hands in surrender)
How can I control your trigger finger?

YOUNG WOMAN: (shrugs)

YOUNG MAN: (takes his hat off)
Then what do we do? Arm the population?
Wear Kevlar to the Cineplex?

YOUNG WOMAN:
Now that would be a dream deferred.

(hands YOUNG MAN the gun)

YOUNG MAN: Talk about a heavy load.

(weighs it, points it at her)

YOUNG WOMAN: Whoa!

YOUNG MAN: Or does it explode?

(points it at us)

END OF PLAY

ORANGUTANS DON'T KILL

By Winter Miller

[Winter Miller's plays include *Paternity, The Penetration Play,* and *The Arrival*.
In Darfur was the recipient of The Guthrie Theater and Playwrights' Center's Two-Headed Challenge 2006 commission under the mentorship of New York Times journalist and Pulitzer winner Nicholas Kristof and developed at the Guthrie Theater, the Playwrights Center Playlabs, Geva Theater's Hibernatus Interruptus and The Public Theatre's New Works Now. *In Darfur* inaugurated the Public's Lab series in April 2007 for a sold out three week run, and filled to capacity a staged reading at the 1800-seat Delacorte Theater on July 9th, 2007. Simultaneously, on July 9th, the Donmar Warehouse held a reading. The Tricycle Theater held a reading in December 2007, for A Day for Darfur. As a journalist, Ms. Miller has reported for the *New York Times, New York Magazine* and *Variety* among others. A graduate of Smith College, she holds an MFA in playwriting from Columbia University. She is a founding member of the Obie-winning 13Playwrights (13P), a member of the Playwrights Union, the Dramatist Guild and a New Georges Affiliated Artist.]

*

The other day I walked past a mosquito with the mind of a killer, she was holding up a five & dime store with a Beretta blue semi-automatic,

held it tight to the clerk's head, mosquito said, One step and I slug you,

Now, the county records revealed this same dame was a victim of ancestral circumstance, her great aunt Elisabeth was taken hostage by a gang of caterpillars wielding back-alley traded AK-47's, the tragedy was, a rival gang of cats came after those caterpillars with some shiny-ass Smith & Wessons and shot those caterpillars down in their primes,

those caterpillars never got to be butterflies, they got caught up in the wrong thing at the right time or the right thing at the wrong time--no one could deduce because it was all so fast,

Still, everyone in town (except Jennifer) knew the cats and the caterpillars had a long-standing beef and the only way it was going to turn out was if one side was decimated, which pissed the hell out of the fine young zebras who lived one suburb over and kept their coats pristine and their minds clean by reading Emerson, Thoreau and Zora Neale Hurston and they couldn't and wouldn't arm

themselves, them zebras said it's a credo and they knit wool sweaters, sang glorious hymns and protested any infraction against any living thing,
But there was a day, it was a Thursday according to the calendar, that one orangutan snapped because his breakfast was cold, his pa didn't respect him, and he'd never be able to afford the right sneakers or hold the right job and he heard voices say, take the zebras out and he knew what he had to do. He had his heart set on an M16 from Vietnam but this kid didn't have the grease, all he could get with his mama's charge card was an AR-15,
                    but what of it?
        Because online he met a goat who knew a freshwater salmon loaded to the gills--300 rounds left over from an aborted spree in a recently colonized country! The orangutan palmed a Happy Meal from Mcdonald's and mailed a birthday card to his most beloved teacher with a note he wrote: When I fall, I fall with dignity, these zebras were a menace, poisoning the minds of our children, polluting the land. I will be exalted, I will be remembered.

HAPPINESS

By Chiori Miyagawa

[Chiori Miyagawa is a NYC-based playwright, a resident playwright at New Dramatists, and a core member of NoPassport. Her plays have been produced off-Broadway, at renowned performance houses in NYC and regionally. A collection of seven of her plays, Thousand Years Waiting and Other Plays, is published by Seagull Books; and another collection of five plays, America Dreaming and Other Plays is published by NoPassport Press. She is a recipient of many fellowships including a New York Foundation for the Arts Playwriting Fellowship, a McKnight Playwriting Fellowship, a Rockefeller Bellagio Residency Fellowship, and a Radcliffe Institute for Advanced Study Fellowship at Harvard University. Chiori teaches playwriting at Bard College where she created an undergraduate playwriting program under the chair JoAnne Akalaitis.]

*

Character: A white woman in her 20s.
Time: Now
Place: Suburban U.S.A.

Notes: If possible, I'd like the woman to have a pink baby stroller. I would prefer he not to hold a fake baby or lift a bundle up from the stroller at any point. Her monologue should be read in a pleasant, friendly, and sincere manner all the way through with no trace of malice. We like her very much until nearly the end of her monologue.

YOUNG WOMAN: All mothers think their daughter is beautiful, but everyone says that about my daughter. Strangers come up to me and give me compliments when I'm out strolling with her. It must be my husband's genes, because I'm no beauty. I do take credit for dressing her nicely. She really does look like an angel on the Sistine Chapel ceiling or something. Except of course, she wears clothes. Adorable baby clothes. I read somewhere that fifty percent of your happiness is inherited. The level of your happiness, if you made absolutely no effort to be happy, is determined by your genes. That leaves you fifty percent to do something about. I'm basically a happy person, and my husband is an optimistic man. So I'd say my daughter's starting point for being happy is pretty good. It's my job to make sure that she gains the skills to fill in her part of the fifty percent.

A lot of people strive for success or wealth, but in reality, those things don't make you happy. Money makes people unhappy if anything, and fame makes people crazy. Family makes you happy. Helping others and doing good for your community makes you happy. I don't want my daughter to grow up exceptional. I'm fine with her being an ordinary good person. But it's not going to be easy if she keeps growing more and more beautiful. I grew up in this town. When I was in high school, there were many beautiful girls on the cheerleading team. I tried out once because I was a decent gymnast, but I didn't make it. It turned out to be a positive outcome though. My husband, who was a football star, didn't want to have anything to do with cheerleaders. He wanted an ordinary girl. I got lucky. I do worry about my daughter on that aspect. I'm not bragging; she is really a gorgeous baby. She's my life's achievement so far. I'm going to be a good mother always, as long she needs me. Beautiful women are vulnerable. That's why it's important that as a mother, I do the right thing. My husband agrees with me. We agree on everything. We're lucky that way. I'm going to prepare my daughter for her fifty percent of happiness that she has to cultivate when she grows up.

It's our constitutional right to pursue happiness. My beautiful daughter makes me happy. I'm a gun owner, so I can protect her. I'll teach her that no one should take her guns away. It's her constitutional right to have it. If you're a mother and you love your family, you must agree with me. The borders are not secure, and numerous criminals occupy this country. Even if you live in a safe neighborhood, you can't prevent them from coming to you. Once they're in, you can't make them go back to where they came from. The government, which is supposed to protect us, will do nothing.

Do not give up your freedom. It's your constitutional right. It's your children's constitutional right. I know you understand me because you believe in certain values. Because you love your children, too.

She smiles warmly.

Excerpt from *the nature of captivity*

by
matthew paul olmos

[Matthew Paul Olmos was most recently
awarded the 2012 Princess Grace Award in
Playwriting and selected as a 2013 Sundance
Institute Resident Playwright at UCROSS. He
was also named, by Sam Shepard, as the
inaugural recipient of the La MaMa e.t.c.'s
Ellen Stewart Emerging Playwright Award. He
is a 2012-13 New York Theatre Workshop
Fellow, previous Sundance Institute Time
Warner Storytelling Fellow, 2012-13 Primary
Stages Dorothy Strelsin New American
Writer's Group playwright; Rising Circle
Collective writer, Brooklyn Arts Exchange
Resident Artist and a two-time Resident Artist
at Mabou Mines/Suite. He received the BBC
International Playwriting Top Prize of the
Americas for his play THE NATURE OF
CAPTIVITY. For more information:
www.matthewpaulolmos.com. This work was
developed in part in the
Resident Artists Program 2009-10 and 2010-11
of Mabou Mines/*SUITE,* mentored by Ruth
Maleczech and Terry O'Reilly.]

*

Part I – the outside

characters
Justus, Nellie, Lulu
& Gooch

place
anywhere

time
just before progress

"Now Tom Said; 'Ma, whenever there's a cop beatin' a guy
Wherever a hungry new born baby cries
Where there's a fight against the blood and hatred in the air
Look for me Ma, I'll be there
Wherever somebody fightin' for a place to stand
For a decent job or a helpin' hand
Wherever somebody strugglin' to be free
Look in their eyes Ma, you'll see me.'"
-Bruce Springsteen, The Ghost of Tom Joad

*

A salvaged room.

LULU: Nellie?
JUSTUS: You okay, Nellie?

LULU: Nellie, c'mon, of course that's not why.
JUSTUS: Breathe, Nellie.
NELLIE: …
LULU: Nellie?
NELLIE: …

(NELLIE weeps)

NELLIE: …how…how could you go out there,
Lu, you don't have to go with them, …there's
horrible things out there, ….how could
anyone…?

(A single, crystal gunshot is heard from just
outside, A bit of commotion/voices. Lights focus to
NELLIE)

NELLIE: If I was a bullet…I'd be so proud.
Always when I hear them go off, even from
that very first time….always I imagine.
(pause) They sit, inside the gun machine. So
warm and snug. Other little bullets snug next
to them.

(NELLIE acts like a bullet)

NELLIE: (to other bullets) Hey. Hi. Warm in
here, isn't it?
An I bet you they don't wanna go. In fact, I bet
you they would stay inside that gun machine
for all their lives, just sitting, like this. (pause)

But I guess that's not what bullets were invented for. Staying put. (pause) They have to go somewhere. Out. Into the world. But know why it'd be okay to be a bullet? Cuz yougettogososofast! (pause) So fast they move that I wanna SCREAM! (pause) And finally, they're someplace else.

(GOOCH appears close to NELLIE, she lands in him. There is blood coming out of his chest. NELLIE backs away, scared)

NELLIE: But a bullet doesn't know where he or she is going. They just go. Because somebody makes them so. Somebody makes them. So they go. I don't think anyone should be made to go anywhere. You should only go where you want to. Bad stuff happens when forced to go. Bad stuff happens. Like that.

(GOOCH crumples to the floor, wounded. Spotlight ends)

LULU: Omigod, Gooch....

(All surround GOOCH, trying to help)

JUSTUS: Nellie, get me some water then I need ya ta put pressure right here. (pause) Nellie, go!

(NELLIE does)

JUSTUS: Lu, you talk to him, let him hear your voice. (pause) Lu!

(JUSTUS digs into the wound, NELLIE pours water)

LULU: Hey there, Gooch, it's me. Lulu. Yea, I'm right here close. Just like you always wanted. With you an not goin'no place. Can you hear me?

(GOOCH joins LULU downstage, while the JUSTUS/NELLIE still tend to his body lying on the floor upstage)

GOOCH: Of course, I can hear you, you're talkin'into my ear, love.
LULU: I shouldn'tve sent you out.
GOOCH: You didn't send me, I went.
LULU: I'm sorry, Gooch, sometimes I am *so* sorry.
GOOCH: Just sometimes?
LULU: …how are ya feelin', Gooch?
GOOCH: Well, your brother is trying to dig a bullet out of my chest. I've felt better.
LULU: How did—

GOOCH: Doesn't matter. They woulda got me soon enough, I always come by here at night. To make sure you're okay. That you're safe.

LULU: ...I didn't know that.

GOOCH: Every night.

LULU: Who was—

GOOCH: They all look alike to me. (pause) You don't though, you look one-of-a-kind. Holding over me. My God, look at you. If there was anything ever I wanted to be lookin' at while my breathin' stopped....it's you.

LULU: You shouldn't talk like that.

GOOCH: It's true. You're it for me.

LULU: Even when you're at the heap today?

GOOCH: (smiling) You shoulda seen the smell.

LULU: I can imagine.

GOOCH: Know something? (pause) They all smell like that when they're not you.

(LULU looks back at where his body is; worried)

NELLIE: Jus, what's wrong, how come he's shivering like that for?

JUSTUS: Means he's givin' a fight, Nel. I just need ta git it...if I can just...

(JUSTUS digs further)

LULU: You never give up, do you?

GOOCH: If you don't have what you want, what else have you got.

LULU: They're closeby then?

GOOCH: Yea, this is about the last spot left.

JUSTUS: Come on!

NELLIE: Easy, Jus, you don't wanna bury it in further.

(JUSTUS slips, NELLIE has trouble holding GOOCH down)

NELLIE: That's too much blood, too much.

LULU: Hey, lookit me.

(LULU holds GOOCH's face)

NELLIE: You see me?

GOOCH: Oh yea.

LULU: You can do this. You just keep not'givin'up like how you do with me. You hear me.

JUSTUS: He's lost too much.

NELLIE: No, keep tryin, keep tryin'.

JUSTUS: I...I don't know much else I can do.

GOOCH: I think this is it, Lu. I think that's clear.

LULU: No. You're wrong. You're gonna stay the night here, with me. Just like how you

always dreamed. Layin' right up close. You'll
be wrapped around me like…
GOOCH: You don't have to—
LULU: Shut up. Wrapped around me like…
GOOCH: Like death, Lu?

*(LULU kisses GOOCH. Meanwhile JUSTUS
stands back up, all staring at the body)*

JUSTUS: I can't do nothin' more
NELLIE: But…
JUSTUS: Was too deep.
NELLIE: Is he…oh god, is he…
JUSTUS: Yea. He is, Nellie.

*(LULU and GOOCH finish their kiss. GOOCH
looks back at his now lifeless body)*

GOOCH: I got to go.
LULU: No, please. Just…
GOOCH: C'mon, Lu, don't make my last sight
be you cryin'.
LULU: I'm sorry all the time for how I was.
I'm sorry I wasn't nicer.
GOOCH: Hey, you were honest. And you're
here now.
LULU: But—
GOOCH: Hey Lu.
LULU: What?

GOOCH: I'm happy. Right at the end…I am.
Cuz of you.
LULU: I'm goin'miss you, Gooch. I will. I do.
GOOCH: Know what? I believe you.

*(GOOCH memorizes her neck, then returns to his
body)*

JUSTUS: Know what he'd say if he could still
speak? (pause) "On my last day, I got to give
it good an hard to some nameless piece in the
morning, and by night I was bein' kissed by
the one I love and always will." That's a pretty
good day.
NELLIE: Least he never was up on that heap,
least he had that.
JUSTUS: They ain't gonna get no more bodies
on that heap. They've had their last.
LULU: I don't know if I'm cryin'over him, like
who he was…or that I'll never be as beautiful
again as…
JUSTUS: It's good that you are, Lu, cryin'.
He'd appreciate.
NELLIE: How come they gunshot him, what'd
he do?
JUSTUS: He was here. That's all it takes.
LULU: They'll be here soon. They will.

(A beat. Lights close-in on NELLIE)

NELLIE: I know I said earlier how I'd wanna be a bullet
but... honest, I don't really understand the gun machine.
like why it was invented for.
like I've never even seen one. Just only heard how loud. (pause)
I imagine the gun machine to be very, very heavy.
And if I were to touch it...it'd be so hot, probably burn my...

(Illustrates her hand)

NELLIE: It's got metal, I know that much. And it's fast, like I was saying. And it does that...

(Illustrates GOOCH's body)

NELLIE: ...that much I know real good.
I guess I don't understand what they need them for. I mean I get it that they need them to put the bullets go realreal fast. But...why do they even wanna do that?
Why did they bring them along on that boat thing when they got here? What were they expecting to find that they'd need mean things like that for? And *before* they got here, what did they do with them? Did they make the

gun machines go loud on each other, on their own kind?

I got so many questions I'd like to know the answers to, but... maybe I'm better off, maybe I haven't got the mind to understand anyways. And maybe, oh this might sound awful to say, but maybe I wish their boat thing had sunk down into the cold, cold ocean before they ever landed on our nice-place-ta-live.

(JUSTUS joins NELLIE in her light)

JUSTUS: C'mon, Nellie.

NELLIE: Couldn't we just stay here a little longer, huh Jus? Oh, it's so peaceful here, so quiet.

JUSTUS: You will, Nellie. Pretty soon you'll be able to stay like this an nobody will take you from it. But right now, I need you to come back. C'mon, Nellie.

(Lights back to all)

GUN CULTURE

By Ian Rowlands

[Ian Rowlands originally trained as an actor at
the Welsh College of Music and Drama. To
date, he has been the Artistic Director of four
theatre companies, most recently North Wales
Stage which specialised in multi lingual /
disciplinary work. As a dramatist, he has
written many plays / films including - A Light
in the Valley for the BBC (Dir. Michael
Bogdanov - Winner of Royal TV Society
Award) and in theatre, the award winning
Marriage of Convenience , *Blue Heron in the Womb*
, *Pacific* , *Butterfly, Blink* - which, has was
produced at 59E59 as part of the Brits Off
Broadway season 2008.]

*

I was sitting in Thompson House - one time
home of the inventor of a very efficient sub-
machine gun - sipping a bottle of Kentucky
Bourbon Barrel Ale. The Mount Pleasant String
Band pickin' and dancin' like bluegrass moths
around a retro mic; just another Summer
evening in the Tri-state.

Next morning I caught a Greyhound down to
Dayton, where the Accord was signed, I was
on my way to Troy, Ohio, But when I arrived

at Dayton, turns out, there was no way for me to get there. "No bus?" "No bus" "No train?" "No train" "But Troy is a city of twenty thousand!" You just don't go there" "Right..." " Well you could call a cab, but that'd cost you a hundred and fifty bucks" "Hundred and fifty bucks!" I nearly got on that Greyhound and headed back to banks of the Ohio! When this black guy said "I'll take you there" His name was Jesse – great guy, without him I would not have reached the Square; sure as hell I wouldn't be here now telling you why I wanted to get there; Jesse was a real gentleman. "One question", he asked of me "Why?"

Why, Troy? "Yeah... why?" That's one hell of a question... Well, sir, I said, One morning, a few years back, I was teaching at a small college in Ohio, when a colleague came in; a great guy; wherever he went, he brought the sun with him. You know that kind of guy; so positive – just, not that morning. Turns out, the night before, his nephew, a crack sniper who'd just come home on leave from Iraq, was showing his new high velocity rifle to his pa, when his pa accidentally pulled the trigger and shot his son dead" "God damn" "Yeah...anyway, as I listened to the account of that boy's death, I just kept thinking about his ma – wondering whether she'll be able to lie next to her husband ever again; to lie next to the man who killed her only son? That's the problem with being a writer, Jesse - inspiration. It's invariably won at the expense of someone else's misery! Now I know I shouldn't have been thinking such selfish thoughts, at the time, Jesse, but I was" "God has his reasons" "Yeah, he sure does..."

"Anyway, years pass and I'm back in NY teaching The Trojan Women. Do you know the Trojan Women, Jesse?" "No" No?, it's an old play about war and shit.... and it was around the time of the thousandth US casualty of our 'Holy Crusade', and I was thinking about little boys games and their effect upon women, when suddenly, I put the theme of that play and the shooting of that boy together and I think, 'Adaptation!' My little protest against these interesting times, I'll adapt the Trojan Women and I'll set it in a Troy, USA of today.

So I start Googling. I knew there was a Troy, NY State and a Troy, Michigan, but I was hoping there'd be a Troy Ohio, because Ohio's is Winesburg country! And you know what, Jesse, there <u>was</u> a God!" "Hell I know that, kid, otherwise I wouldn't know where the hell we're goin'!" Jesse said "Yeah, sure, but that's why, Sir, that's why I want to get there; to write a play - about guns and America..." And

Jesse turned to me, and he said "Does Troy know you're comin'?" And I just smiled at him, and... and by then, we'd reached the Square. So, Jesse dropped me off and promised to pick me up in a few days, and there I was, alone in the heart of Troy, heart of America; spiritual home of mac 'n cheese and apple pie!

So, I check into the Hampton Inn and I turn on the TV and there, on the news was a story about an eight year old boy from Vandalia... turns out he'd just shot his pa dead whilst his pa was teaching him how to shoot a gun. And, to my shame, the writer in me thought, "Huzzah!" Thank god, the father in me was more redeeming, and I screamed at the TV "Why! The 2nd amendment was only written to kill the God damn British! That was two hundred fuckin' years ago! Ok I'm being simplistic, but that's why there's this gun shit. Can we move on? Can we put the gun down? Now? Because it's already too late!' Later that evening, in a bar, across the road from the Courthouse, where the convicted shoot hoops in a caged court, there was no bluegrass, no joy; the silence took away my taste for beer. And as I walked along the Interstate back to the hotel, I looked up at the wide Ohio skies and I swear I heard the scream of a mother and the cry of a young boy blowin' across the plains..

A POEM FOR SANDY HOOK

By August Schulenburg

[August's plays include *Carrin Beginning, Kidding Jane, Rue, Riding the Bull, Good Hope, Other Bodies, Honey Fist, Dark Matter, Jacob's House, DEINDE, Dream Walker, Denny and Lila, Dark Matter, Jane the Plain* and *The Lesser Seductions of History*. His plays have been produced and developed at The Lark, Bay Area Playwrights Festival, Chelsea Playhouse, Theater for the New City, Portland Stage Company, Dayton Playhouse, Colonial Players, Pennsylvania Shakespeare Festival, Contemporary Stage Company, Abingdon Theater Company, Gideon Productions, New Amerikan Theatre, Penobscot Theatre, Impetuous Theater Group, Decades Out, Soundtrack Series, Reverie Productions, Wolf 359, Blue Box Productions, Piper McKenzie, Boomerang Theatre Company, Adaptive Arts, Hall High School, Nosedive Productions, MTWorks, Purple Repertory, Valley Repertory Company, The Brick Theater, CAPS LOCK Theatre, Chameleon Theatre Circle, Retro Productions, Elephant Run District and Flux Theatre Ensemble, where he is the Artistic Director. His work has also been published in the New York Theater Review, Stage and Screen, Indie Theater Now, Midway Journal,

and in two issues of Carrier Pigeon. He also
writes for film and television with
MozzleStead Productions.]

*

After the upturned desks, the hiding in closets,
the running and
The no time to run; after the lines of red-eyes
and open mouths,
The microphones pressed in the faces of
children but
Not all of them; after crying in the far office
bathroom
For kids I'll never know in a place I've never
been, again;
After the petitions and tweets and posts
And speeches and hearts going out out out
again,
After the never-again, again;
Again it will happen, in Damascus and
Panjwai,
In Columbine and Oakland and other places
Named for trees and flowers; again the
promises and laws
Will blossom and fall like trees and flowers,
and the kids,
Like trees, like flowers, will be too beautiful to
bear but
They will be, borne to places under ordinary
grass.

After the grass and the stones on stones, after the name
Of the man with the gun is spoken for the last time,
After there are no words must come the words,
Because there are words and you know you know them,
I do, even if I don't know how to say them.
They are the words welling up in my eyes as I
Picture the backpacks and crayons; words like cool rain
On scalded minds, words like rivers over dusty laws,
Words that shake my body when I hold you close,
(And I am, right now, holding you close), words
We bury under ordinary grass, because we are busy
And afraid and polite and the jerk in the checkout line
And the asshole in the traffic and the inconvenience
Of all the what were we talking about again? and then,
Tomorrow, another after.
After another after,
I must say rain and river,
After never-again again,
I must sing of backpacks and crayons;
After there are no words,

We must make new ones,
Words fashioned from the sounds
Children make when
They collide in bright-eyes and bruised-knees
On playgrounds,
Words that don't wait
To make the world
What we say it is
When we say
This is what the world is
To children.

HURT

By Saviana Stanescu

[Saviana Stanescu is a Romanian-born award-winning playwright. Her work has been widely presented internationally and in the US. Recent productions include "For a Barbarian Woman" (a co-production Fordham/EST directed by Niegel Smith), "Aliens with extraordinary skills" at Women's Project (published by Samuel French), "Bechnya" at Hudson Theatre in LA, "Waxing West" (2007 New York Innovative Theatre Award for Outstanding Full-length Script) at La MaMa Theatre. "Bucharest Underground" won the 2007 Marulic Prize for Best European Radio-Drama. In Stockholm, Sweden, Saviana's play "White Embers" produced by Dramalabbet made it in the TOP 3 of Best Plays in 2008, and in NYC is published by Samuel French as one of their 2010 OOB festival winners. Ms Stanescu has published books of poetry and drama including "The New York Plays", "Aliens With Extraordinary Skills", "Waxing West", "Google me!", "Black Milk" and "The Inflatable Apocalypse" (Best Play of the Year UNITER Award in 2000). She co-edited the anthology of plays "Global Foreigners" (with NYU professor Carol Martin) and "roMANIA after 2000" (with CUNY professor Daniel Gerould). <u>www.saviana.com</u>]

*

DARKO – 40s, depressed handsome man speaking with a strong Serbian accent
LAURA – early 30s, cute American woman, girlish, insecure, lonely, big-hearted
TANYA – 18, spunky yet vulnerable student living with her single Croatian mother

A one-bedroom apartment in Brooklyn.

Darko, in a business suit and slippers, talks to the audience like to a video camera.

His briefcase is on the floor. His cell phone rings.

DARKO: *(his cell phone rings; and rings)* I'm not gonna answer. I hope you all know that cell phones are bad for your health. Brain cancer is closer than you think. But we don't see that, we don't, because radiation is invisible, electromagnetic waves are invisible... and sometimes even people, people can be invisible too.
LAURA: *(talking to her cat, Penelope)* He didn't ask if I had a pet. But I did, I told him I had a cat. I even mentioned your name – Penelope. He wasn't very good at small talk. He went on a rant about the danger of cell phones. Then he

took my hand, made a "cell phone" out of it and whispered: "this is not just a date for me, it's a special encounter, a gift from God, a randomly emerged union of two complementary particles called SOULS".

DARKO: I'm a good Christian. I believe in goodness, I believe in honesty, I believe in people. But they all disappointed me. Deeply. I still believe in the beauty of a mathematical solution. A neat gorgeous proof. Numbers. Facts. CORPSES. I believe in God.

You might say it's a contradiction here. It's not. Science, mathematics, are just forms in which God has organized this world. God's algorithms are not to be revealed so easily to mortals. Except for the moments when they are close to DEATH.

TANYA: Sit down, mom, and don't interrupt me, please. I gotta tell you something kinda important. I mean not important-important, like it's not about our lives or something. No, it's not about money. I didn't get expelled from school. Don't worry. I'm not sick, nothing like that. No, I'm not pregnant!

LAURA: OK, he's not in my league, you'd say. He's a professor. Why would you say that? I'm more well-cultured than all the girls I know! I read a lot. I listen to NPR. I'm a walking wikipedia, but you wouldn't know that, you're a stupid cat!

DARKO: For years I had to pretend everything was fine. Why bother complaining? I tried once and <u>they</u> didn't even listen to what I had to say, they told me I had an "unhealthy" attitude. What is a "healthy fuckin' attitude"? A robot following their rules? An ass-kisser? A hypocrite? Another expert in the sucking-up game?

LAURA: He called me "dangerously beautiful"… That doesn't happen everyday. It might actually never happen again.

I shouldn't have said that stupid thing about not shaving my legs… because I actually did. I did shave my legs before our date, or whatever, our "special encounter".

DARKO: They found a so-called reason, of course. They said a freshman student complained about my teaching methods. Bullshit. The students love me. Read my evaluations!

(cell phone rings, and rings)

DARKO: Creditors. They ring and ring and fuckin' ring. I feel like killing this fuckin' cell phone. But I can't. Yet. It's my only gate to the world. I haven't paid it for the last 3 months but it still rings. Stubborn motherfucker! ConEd just cut my electricity. Luckily my video camera has damn good batteries! *(laughs weirdly)* Soon it will be dark. Darko will be in the dark!

TANYA: OK, would you just listen, please, mom? Please, just listen. This time, just listen! I did somethink kinda weird. OK, maybe even wrong. And I'm not sure why I did it, but... OK, it's like... this professor we have... had... Darko Rasnin... yeah, a Serbian guy, but he lived here like forever, like you, since '93 or something.

DARKO: *(the cell phone starts ringing again – he takes a look at the caller ID)* The landlord. She's a good woman, from China. Her patience has a limit too. I don't blame her. I haven't paid the rent in 4 months. EVICTION is written in big letters on my forehead. Homelessness - a new start. Bankruptcy – another great start. Amazing new beginnings await for me. Fucking bullshit capitalist propaganda.

LAURA: Yes, he knows I'm a lab technician, he was OK with that. He's a scientist! And it's not like I'm doing something shameful! Someone has to work on those STD tests too. I actually like this job much more than working at the hospital, we already discussed that. Too many people over there. We like the quiet time: just you, purring, me, thinking... a few test tubes around are OK, but people, too many people are not OK.

DARKO: You may ask why don't I take a job, another job, any kind of job.

I did. I worked as a scientific advisor for the Environmental Health Trust, a public health institution that examines the health impact of environmental exposures. Did you see that NY Times article about the impact of cell phones? I was quoted in it. I spoke about their health effects and social implications. Didn't you notice those couples in a restaurant, on a romantic evening, each of them texting someone else... People don't connect with each other anymore. You invite a woman for a romantic dinner and she's freakin' texting between two bites... Women don't know how to connect with men anymore. And men don't know how to connect with women. Shall I be polite, shall I open the door for her or will she hit me on my head with her purse?

LAURA: I really dressed well for that date, I did. Classy restaurant. I could tell from the name: Marseilles. French. He has good taste.

DARKO: I don't understand women anymore. You want to make her feel good, you don't have lots of money but you book a fancy dinner at a super-fancy restaurant in Chelsea, you bring her roses, you ooze sex appeal and desire and interest in her, you pay the bill, and what does she do? She accuses you of sexual harassment. She's "not ready" to do it yet. She doesn't want to be "pushed". She wants to wait for the "right moment". She didn't shave her legs to make sure she doesn't respond to

your erotic advances on the first date. You
know what, go fuck yourself, Laura!
LAURA: How many days have passed? A
week. And he didn't call, he didn't.
I only told him he shouldn't sexually harass
me, that's all I said. Like a joke, you know.
Well, half a joke. I wasn't ready to…
I need to first erase all those beautiful Latin
names of STDs from my mind before… I mean,
he should understand this – you can't work on
STD tests all day long and then jump into it.
Sex, I mean.
DARKO: Yes, you're pretty, and you didn't
text messages at the table, but you don't get
me. We could have had something beautiful
together. Darko and Laura. A family. Kids. A
house full of laughter. Like you see in those
stupid American romantic comedies. We could
have had all that. And more. You fucking
spoiled everything!
LAURA: He doesn't take rejection well, I could
see that in his eyes. His eyelashes were like…
biting the air. His mouth was so sad, his lips…
/ Anyway.
DARKO: Anyway… That NY Times article was
dynamite. Mom framed it. The internet
version. She shows it to all our neighbors. She's
really proud of me. No, she doesn't understand
English, but she can see my name printed in
the paper.

LAURA: Yes, I know. I'm a loser. I shouldn't let a man like Darko go. Chivalric men are an endangered species. You don't need to hide under the bed to make your point, Penelope. Of course he gave me his number!

(Darko's cell phone rings; and rings)

DARKO: Mom doesn't know. I got fired after that article. I couldn't find any other job in my field. But I still have dignity and prestige! I'm not a human Kleenex. I told them the emperor was naked. *(I was fine – in Serbian)* Bio sam u redu.

(He opens his briefcase and takes a handgun out of it. He loads the semi-automatic pistol.)

TANYA: OK, so… he's like, in class, and after class, he's like you know talking to me in Serbian, although I told him we don't speak Serbian at home, I told him you're Bosnian… But no, he's like talking to me in Serbian, and that's like so embarrassing, like Julie asked me like why don't you answer him in Yugoslavian, or whatever language you guys speak over there in the Balkans… And I'm like, I'm not from the Balkans, my mom is, I was raised here, and she's like "whatever". And then Jessica is like "you guys are Muslim?" And I'm like my mom is Muslim but I'm not,

I'm an atheist, I don't believe in that religion shit, that's only to control the masses. And she's like "whatever". And Patrick is like "Serbians are Christian, Bosnians are Muslim, that's why they fought against each other in the Balkan war, isn't that so, Tanya? And I'm like "whatever".

DARKO: 9x19mm Grandpower K100 Slovak semi-automatic pistol. The best.

TANYA: OK, so that kinda discussion, or variations of it, I had like each time we had a class with that freakin' Darko… so I was like, couldn't take it anymore… and one day, when I had the monthly meeting with my academic advisor, I was like telling her: our Intro to IT professor Darko Rasnin, you know… I'm sorry to have to say this… his teaching methods are… I mean, he's a little sexist, he was kinda… you know, I kinda feel like he was like kinda flirting with me… I feel a little sexually harassed, yes… No, he didn't touch me or anything… but the way he looks at me, and he always keeps me after class to talk to me in Serbian… I mean, yes, we both have Balkan roots, but that doesn't make it OK to… I mean, my mom was gang-raped by the fuckin' Serbians and I just can't, I can't have him look at me like that!

DARKO: *(holding the gun in his hands)*
So here's the plan. I have nothing to lose, have I? Actually there's a lot to win: fame. Posterity

will know my name. Yes, in connection to a killing spree, but who cares. Fame is fame. Bad publicity is good publicity too. People will know my name. Write books about me. Make movies. Win Oscars. And after my name is known by millions, that's when they will look at my interview and see what I had to say about the danger of cell phones. A controversial discussion will escalate. Globally. The "darko" effect will be in everyone's mind when they speak on a cell phone. And they speak on cell phones all the time. They speak like they breathe. All of them. Everybody on this planet will know Darko's name and the ideas he died for.

TANYA: I know you don't want me to talk about that anymore. But that doesn't change the way I feel, mom. I'm not doing well with anger management when it comes to Serbians. Why did he have to talk with me in Serbian? I mean, when I had that guy Marko in class for a semester in high school, it was kinda OK, he never talked to me in Serbian.

Even if we don't talk about this, mom, it doesn't change the fact that I am a rape-child, I'm the product of that freakin' rape, mom, I'm the daughter of a gang of motherfuckin' Serbians! And if we don't talk about this, mom, you're not gonna heal, and I'm not gonna heal, and we can't move on, I can't move on, I wanna deal with this, mom!

(A cell phone rings; and rings)

LAURA: *(calling Darko)* He's not answering. Of course. Why should he? I bet he found another woman. Well. Better like this. What can I tell him? That I changed my mind and now, after a week, I kinda am in the mood for…
I can't tell him that. Maybe I can. Why not? I gotta learn to be more direct. When I want something I gotta say it. Yes, I will say it. If he gives me the chance. If he answers the phone. No. He won't. *(she hangs up)* Why am I talking about him "giving me a chance"?
Do we still have Dr Phil's book, "Self matters"? OK. Let's work on my self-esteem. I tend to wait for validation from other people. Or cats! That's not good. That's eating me. I must find my authentic self. Create my life from inside out. How does Dr Phil put it? "I am asking you to call a huge time-out from this scramble you call life, and to focus on the one doing the scrambling: you."
DARKO: In some countries I'd be a hero. Here I'm gonna be called a crazy terrorist. It's OK. It's still worth taking the risk. There's nothing to lose. I will die with a little dignity. Shouting at those hypocrites: "Adjuncts! You're all adjuncts! Adjuncts of human beings!"
No, I'm not gonna shout. I'm gonna be very calm. I'm gonna hold the Chair at gunpoint

and I'm gonna talk *(he mimics that talk:)* slowly, clearly, professorially.

TANYA: Yeah, I reported the Serb for sorta sexual-harassment-attempt, and he got fired. He never knew what hit him, they told him that, you know, in this economy, blah, blah... they had to make cuts, to cut some adjuncts. Adjuncts are not like real professors. They are hired like on part-time, no-responsibility basis. So he didn't get any more courses. They kicked him out. After like 15 years of teaching. Part-time teaching.

DARKO: Tomorrow is the monthly faculty meeting at 10 am. They will all be there... Everybody will be there. The "professors".

TANYA: Mom? I kinda feel guilty now. I mean I fucked him up and he didn't really do anything bad to me. Except for speaking in Serbian. But still. He could be one of the bad guys, couldn't he? One of the guys who raped you. He could be my father. Couldn't he?

DARKO: I'm going to enter the building calmly – I still have the university ID. The guard will smile at me and say "what's up, man" as always. A really cool guy, Jamal. He likes me. I like him. We played soccer together on a Sunday, last year. A good guy. Underdog. Born into no-money, bad circumstances. What's up, bro?!
It's down, man. I'm freakin' down. Eating the ground.

TANYA: So I kinda think I should talk to him. If that doesn't completely freak you out. I should try to explain to him, to see if…
I got his address from school. He lives in Brooklyn too. I thought I should let you know. Maybe you see him in the supermarket and it freaks you out. If he's one of them, the bad guys. But maybe he's not. Maybe he didn't even fight in the war. Maybe he was on a fellowship in the US. Maybe he's a good guy… He seemed to know a lot, he seemed to love teaching. I fucked him up, mom. I gotta talk to him.

LAURA: No, we can't afford a therapist this year, but we already know what he will say: work on your self-esteem. Negative internal dialogue has physiological consequences: chronic adrenaline arousal, elevated blood pressure, headaches, depression, low libido… Darko would have helped me. But I didn't let him. Because I'm fucked up and afraid of love. Afraid of people. Who might like me. See the vicious cycle? I gotta break it. I will call him again. And again. Until he answers.

DARKO: I'm leaving all my belongings to Jamal. It's not much, but still. I wrote a last note on this Kleenex *(he shows it):* Jamal is to take all my possessions. No way to have them shipped to mom, back home. No money. No time. Tomorrow is the day. The last day.
I'm not a human Kleenex.

(his cell phone rings; and rings; and rings.)

(Tanya bangs at his door.)

TANYA: Professor?!!

END OF PLAY

THE WAKE

A theatre piece for two or more actors

By Caridad Svich

[Caridad Svich received the 2012 OBIE for
Lifetime Achievement in the Theater and the
2011 American Theatre Critics Association
Primus Prize for her play *The House of the
Spirits*, based on the Isabel Allende novel, and
she has been short-listed for the PEN USA
Award in Drama four times. Among her works
for theatre are *12 Ophelias, Any Place But Here,
Alchemy of Desire/Dead-Man's Blues, Fugitive
Pieces, Iphigenia Crash Land Falls on the Neon
Shell That Was Once Her Heart (a rave fable), In
the Time of the Butterflies (based on the Julia
Alvarez novel), Instructions for Breathing,
GUAPA, Magnificent Waste, The Tropic of X, The
Way of Water* and the multimedia collaboration
The Booth Variations. Her work is published by
Broadway Play Publishing, Eyecorner Press,
TCG, Manchester University Press, Smith &
Kraus, and more. She has edited six books on
theatre and performance. She is alumna
playwright of New Dramatists, founder of
NoPassport theatre alliance and press,
associate editor of Contemporary Theatre
Review for Routledge/UK a Lifetime member
of Ensemble Studio Theatre, and an affiliated

artist with the Lark Play Development Center
in New York City. She holds an MFA in
Theatre from UCSD. Website:
www.caridadsvich.com]

*

We tell ourselves everything's going to be okay
We send prayers up
(even those of us who don't pray)
We wait.

…

Days seem infinite
Cruel
Relentless
In their little offerings of joy.
We curse the days,
Send prayers up
(even those of us who are past prayer now)
And wait.
…

Today, we say,
things will be better.
We will learn.
All hail a better society.

We say this with hope
Sadness

Fear
Doubt
In our throats,
And yet, we still say these words
Because sometimes
There is nothing else.

...

We tear off another page in the calendar.
Mark the days.
It has been these many hours since...
Columbine
Virginia Tech
Aurora
Newtown,

These many minutes since...
Kandahar
Damascus
Karachi
Kashmir...

...

We surf channels
For other stories.

We watch the world's biggest losers
Lose weight,
Bachelors date.
And a child named Honey Boo Boo

Feign a faint.
....

We tweet, text and blog
In hope that someone will
Is
Listening
Somewhere.

And then
In the dark quiet of sleepless night,
We wait.

...

For the pools of blood
Shattered bones
And blasted eyes
To go away.

...

Not here again, we pray
(and this time the prayer is real,
Even if we tell ourselves otherwise).
Not here
Or anywhere else
Ever again, please.

...

But then the drones strike again
Imperceptibly
And there is barely-heard talk of more
Collateral damage
Over there
Far away
From us
Here
Out of harm's way.

...

And we wonder
Is there an end to victory?
Do we chalk up ALL of these losses
To some strange machinery
Brought into being
In the name of democracy?

...

We think these things
In the still dark,
Alone,
Riddled by beads of sweat,
Or strolling through
The international foods aisle
At the supermarket,
As a cart
Carries us forward

Face to face
With the processed meat,
Guava paste,
Fried shrimp crisps
And Heinz baked beans
(Made in England).

And we stop thinking
For a while
And
Dream

Of picture postcards
Travel memoirs
And leisure schemes
Our ancestors told us about
Once
Long ago
In some 'other century.

"Dream train, coming 'round the bend
(mystery train)."
We slip on our headphones
Against the noise of the world,
And bask in Our music.

Yeah.

Our music –

Owned by someone else

In some cloud,
Who can delete it
From us at any time
Without our knowledge.

Yet, we listen anyway
Because Our music
Is safer
Than guns.

...

The calendar shakes.
The days travel in flip-book movies
Of this death, and that videogame
And who is to blame now?

The march of days is cruel,
And we
The tired few
Knotted by grief,
At a loss by loss,
Wait.

...

And wonder
About the unemployed car salesman
From Germany who was kidnapped
By the CIA and spent five months
In the Salt Pit,

After which he was left
At the side of the road in Albania,
And what his life must be like now.

Will any kind of movie ever be made about
him?
Is his story worthy of multinational Hollywood
financing?

Who will tell the story of our lives?

(for a split second
Green Day's "This, This is the time of...")

The cash register reads
$80.29
We don't even know How What...

Pull out the plastic.
It will pay.
Easier that way.

Let's make everything easier.
Right now. Okay?

Let's let the lobbyists push wheedle needle
charm
And curry favor so that THEIR CAUSE makes
the grade.

So what if another million dollars is spent

For a parade/campaign/TV ad/law to push its
way through the hallowed halls of progressive
debt?

These are necessary things, don't you see?

(for a split second
A glimmer of doubt…)

Become necessary, someone says.

The plastic returns to the weary pocket;
The cracked smile holds back tears.
Think: Two guys walked into a bar…

…

It is said:
In hours of despair
There is no room for jokes.
"Bad taste" is the scold;
But how can we even begin
To account for taste
Now
At this stage
Of the piteous game?

Cry:
My brother in Damascus
Is my child in Newtown.

Shout:
My sister in Kandahar
Is my nephew in Aurora.

Whisper:
My future husband in Columbine
Will be my lover one day in Gaza.

..

This gun killed them.
The same gun.

GUN CONTROL
(Excerpted from "Embrace")

By Chris Weikel

[Chris Weikel recently completed his MFA in playwriting at Hunter College, studying under Tina Howe and Mark Bly, and was honored to be one of six playwrights selected to participate in the Kennedy Center ACTF/NNPN MFA Playwrights Workshop in July of 2012. His play SECRET IDENTITY was featured this fall during "Playwright's Week" at the Lark Play Development Center in NYC. His PENNY PENNIWORTH, which according to The New York Times "deserves to become a staple" was produced Off-Broadway by Emerging Artists Theatre Company (EAT) and published by Dramatic Publishing. Weikel is a founding member of TOSOS which presented his PIG TALE: AN URBAN FAERIE STORY in New York as well as at the Absolut Dublin International Gay Theatre Festival. Weikel was commissioned by American Stage Company (St. Petersburg, FL) to write an adaptation of Dylan Thomas's A CHILD'S CHRISTMAS IN WALES for the company's 2000 season. Chris is a judge-at-large for the New York Innovative Theatre Awards and a regular contributor to Drunken! Careening! Writers! at KGB. Chris was a 2008-09 Dramatist Guild Fellow, the 2007 recipient of the Robert Chesley Award for emerging gay playwrights, the 2008 recipient of the Irv Zarkower Award, and a 2011 recipient of the Rita and Burton Goldberg Award.]

*

BILLY: You see this? What's it look like to you?

(BILLY takes his key ring out of his pocket and holds up a bottle opener attached to it.)

A bottle opener, right?

That is what it looks like. Yes. You know what this is really? This is really a fully loaded, standard issue, M16A4, equipped with a Knight's Armament Company M5 RAS handguard which allows for the attachment of vertical grips, lasers and other accessories. There was a time I favored the lighter weight M2 which has a three-round burst firing mode, but really nothing can beat this little baby: the fully automatic, M16A4 "MWS" or "Modular Weapon System."

Yeah. Okay. So you're looking at me right now like—No, I acknowledge it's fucked up.

Okay so... after my last tour... I uhm... I wasn't sleeping. I just couldn't... you know... sleep. That whole... close both eyes, blissful release thing? Not happening. I kept seeing.... I kept thinking.... Let's put it this way: nothing felt right. The bed. The house. Nothing felt right.

It wasn't like you're thinking. Like in the movies. Like crazy shit. I just couldn't sleep. I'd pace the ground floor and check the locks a dozen times. Or worse yet, just lie there, staring at the ceiling, fighting off the urge to go downstairs and check the locks a dozen more times. I knew... intellectually... I knew that our neighbors weren't actually Al Qaeda operatives ready to knife us in our sleep, but I just couldn't shake the feeling that we weren't secure. So... I started sleeping with a loaded weapon under my bed. It worked like a charm. Yup. I slept. Like a baby.

My wife on the other hand was another story. She freaked. So I replaced the rifle with my sidearm. Thought it would be... I don't know... less alarming somehow. Still didn't fly with Emily. Our son was a teenager by then, but our daughter was...what? Ten maybe? Anyway I got where she was coming from. I'm not an idiot. So no loaded guns under the bed, and…

You got it. Pacing again. All night. So my wife... who is a very smart lady... came up with this plan. I could have the gun under the bed as long as I kept the ammunition somewhere else. In a drawer close by. Still within reach. And ... it works. I mean I have to do some convincing of myself... you know some mental gymnastics... that having the ammo in a drawer was as good as having a loaded weapon at the ready, but it worked. I'm finally catchin' some z's and so's the wife. Thing is-- she puts a time limit on it, see. She says I'll give you six weeks... or something... and no more gun. So six weeks go by, and the rifle goes back in a locked cupboard. Out comes my grandad's hunting knife. A pretty lethal looking pig-sticker. It goes under the bed. And I have to work again... mental gymnastics again... to convince myself that that knife makes me as safe as my M4. And somehow I do. I convince myself that that knife actually is my M4. So more time goes by and I keep downsizing, y'know. A pen-knife, a mag-light and finally... it took about a year... I worked my way down to this. This. Little. Deadly weapon.

It's fucked up. But I can sleep.

SEE DICK AND JANE GET READY FOR SCHOOL

By Gary Winter

[Gary Winter was a member of (now imploded) OBIE Award winner 13P. His plays have been produced at the Chocolate Factory; defunkt theater; PS 122: The Cherry Lane Alternative; HERE; The Flea Theater and The Brick. Readings and workshops at EST, Geva, Long Wharf, Little Theater, South Coast Rep and Playwrights Horizons. His ten-minute plays, The White Room and Barge have been finalists for ATL's Heideman Award. I Love Neil LaBute was published in Shorter, Faster, Funnier: Comic Plays and Monologues (Vintage Books, summer 2011). His play Daredevil was recently seen at Dixon Place as part of an ongoing collaboration with director Meghan Finn. From 1998 to 2008 Gary volunteered as Literary Manager of the Flea Theater, where he currently helps organize Pataphysics, workshops for playwrights. From 1984-1989 he directed the legendary Scott & Gary Show for cable television, which featured live performances by experimental bands (i.e.- Beastie Boys, Butthole Surfers, Shockabilly). In 2012 the show was screened at The Museum of the Moving Image. Support: The Goldberg Award, Lark Theater Fellow, SEG Voices, The

Puffin Foundation, Dramatists Guild Fellow, Dasha-Epstein Fellow, John Golden Award, MacDowell Colony and YADDO. Awarded a Spielberg Foundation Righteous Persons Fellowship to study Eastern European Jewry in Krakow. MFA-NYU. Author: gary.winter@nyu.edu]

*

CHARACTERS

HELEN: The Mother
GEORGE: The Father
DICK: Their son
JANE: Their daughter.

SETTING
Helen & George's kitchen. The time is the near future

The kitchen of Helen and George's home.

Two school lunchboxes are on the counter. One has boy stuff on it and the other has girly stuff on it. The boxes are like construction worker lunch pails, except more fortified.

HELEN (Off stage): Is he ready?
GEORGE (Off stage): Dick? Dick?
DICK (Off stage): What!
GEORGE (Off stage): Don't "what". Are you ready?
DICK (Off stage): The Velcro is sticking to my hair again!
JANE (Off stage): Mine is backwards! I can't get it to fit right!
HELEN (Off stage): Coming princess.
DICK (Off stage): Owwwww! My haaaaiiiirrr!
GEORGE (Off stage): Coming Dick.

Sound of frantic footsteps and wailing from Dick and Jane.

Helen enters. Starts piling food into the lunch boxes.
The food is MRE's (Meals Ready-to-Eat that the military uses).

George enters.

GEORGE: Ugh. 45 minutes to get them ready. When I was growing up you rolled out of bed, wolfed down your cereal and was out to the bus stop in fifteen minutes.
HELEN: How quaint.
GEORGE: Things were different.

(Pause)

GEORGE (cont'd): We okay on those?
HELEN: Yup. Costco had a huge sale on
MRE'S so I loaded up. We should have enough
to get the kids to high school.
GEORGE: God, those uniforms, Helen…
HELEN: I know I know you don't have to
remind me.
GEORGE: The kids can't move in them.
HELEN: I know, the standard issue was
designed for telephone poles but that's all they
have.

Phone rings. George answers.

GEORGE: Oh hey Phil. Yeah, we're leaving in
ten. Hmmm, oh sure, sure. Yeah we have
room. Bobby can ride in the gun turret. Sure no
sweat. See you in ten.

George hangs up.

HELEN: Bobby needs a ride again?
GEORGE: Yup.
HELEN: Not surprised.

Jane enters.

*She is wearing full body armor, with a pink, Dora
the Explorer theme design.*

*Logos of corporate sponsors decorate the armor:
WNBA, Mattel, Del Monte, Trump Inc., Golden
Nugget Casino, The Gap, Johnson & Johnson, PBS,
U.S. Olympics, Budweiser, Hooters.*

She is so loaded down she walks like a robot.

Jane is bawling.

HELEN: Honey! What is it!?
GEORGE: What happened sweetie? Is the
Kevlar vest pinching you again?
HELEN: Are the kneepads too tight?
GEORGE: I think it's the helmet…
JANE: Nooooooo!
Look what Dick did!

Jane turns around.

*A bull's eye target has been drawn in chalk on the
back of her vest.*

GEORGE: Oh for….Dick! Dick! Not funny
Dick!

George exits the kitchen.

HELEN: C'mon sweetie. It's only chalk.
Mommy will wipe that right off.
JANE (bawling): Dick made me a bull's eye….

HELEN (as they exit): Now c'mon honey, didn't mommy and daddy tell you that your vest would stop almost any bullet?

Jane wails.

George enters with Dick. Dick is dressed in full body army too.

His black body armor has a Transformers design.

Stickers of corporate sponsors are plastered over his armor: The NY Mets, Monsanto, Remington, Wal-Mart, LEGGO, Victoria's Secret, Toys R Us, Yale, Apple, Disneyland, NBC, Viagra.

GEORGE: When your sister comes down you're going to apologize.
DICK (Muffled through the mask): Okay.
GEORGE: What? I didn't hear you.
DICK (Still muffled but louder): Okay.
GEORGE: That's better.

Helen and Jane enter.

DICK (Takes off his mask): I'm sorry I drew a bull's eye target on the back of your bulletproof vest.

JANE: Don't do that ever again.
DICK: I won't. Promise.

Dick puts his mask back on.

GEORGE: Terrific! Now we're all friends again.
HELEN: All-righty. Now it's off to school with you two warriors!

Helen gives them their very heavy lunch boxes.

The phone rings. Helen answers. Listens.

HELEN: Yes, I understand. Of course. Of course. Well, these things are unavoidable.

She hangs up.
GEORGE: What?
HELEN: One of the police snipers called in sick. There's no one to cover the northwest section of the schoolyard. They have to cancel classes.
DICK and JANE: Ohhhhhhhhhhhh…
GEORGE: C'mon kids, you know the rules: No sniper, no school.
JANE: But what if we stay inside the classroom all day!
DICK: Yeah!
HELEN: That's a very smart idea guys, but you still have to walk from the bus to the school, and you have to make the same walk at the end of the day. That means being outside without protection for 53 seconds, two times in

the same day. Do you know how long it takes for a bullet to travel from a gun to your little bodies?

JANE: Not even a second?

DICK: Way less than not even a second?

HELEN: That's right.

GEORGE: Sorry kids. Rules are rules.

DICK and JANE: Awwwwww.

GEORGE: Hey look, now that you're dressed to go out, what would you like to do today?

HELEN: Yes, something fun!

Dick and Jane take their masks off and think about it.

JANE: Shooting range!

DICK: Land mine demolition!

JANE: Shooting range!

DICK: Land mine demolition!

Lights fade as Dick and Jane argue about how they'd like to spend their day off from school.

RIGHT AFTER VIRGINIA TECH
A Performance Rant Anti-Rant

By Laura Zam

[Laura Zam is an award-winning writer and performer. Her solo work has been presented in New York (Ensemble Studio Theatre, The Public Theater, Dixon Place) as well as internationally and regionally (Woolly Mammoth, The Kennedy Center, The National Theatre, and others). Her newest play MARRIED SEX was commissioned by Theater J for their Locally Grown Festival. Through her award-winning touring play COLLATERALLY DAMAGED, Laura raises awareness about contemporary genocide. Laura has published extensively: plays, monologues, essays, and articles. Awards include the Amiri Baraka Literary Prize, an Open Society grant, a Tennessee Williams Fellowship, and an Artist Fellowship from the DC Commission on the Arts and Humanities. Also an arts-healing educator, Laura has worked with trauma survivors internationally, including teens from the Middle East, U.S. military, and survivors of sexual abuse/assault. She has taught at Brown University, UC Berkeley, and others. Laura has an M.F.A. in Playwriting from Brown University. LauraZam.com.]

Right after Virginia Tech, the worst mass shooting in modern history, I began collecting stories. These were tales of subsequent mass shootings popping up (frequently) in my Yahoo news. I'd print these stories then stuff them in a file folder. I called this file something clever like "Guns." I wanted do something about gun violence, to prevent it, but I didn't know what to do except stuffing paper tragedy into a file folder covered in beautiful butterflies.

Right after Virginia Tech, Virginia's governor at the time, Tim Kaine, convened a panel. He wanted to know: How had this massacre happened? Right afterward, a gunman opened fire at a mall in Utah, killing five. His mother was quoted as saying:

(In a thick Bosnian accent)

He was such a good boy. I don't know what happened.

Around the same time, a gunman opened fire in a church parking lot in Colorado. A congregant said:

        (In a think Southern accent)

We don't why this happened.

That same month, a gunman opened fire at a Nebraska shopping mall, killing nine. The

gunman's childhood friend expressed
confusion:
(In a think Midwestern accent)
 How did this possibly happen?

A few months after Virginia Tech, Tim Kaine's
panel finally came out with their report on the
massacre. It explained what had happened and
also why and how. Importantly, it told the
world how such a thing could be prevented
from ever happening again. The culprit,
according to the report, was a breakdown in
communication at the university. Of the
documents 260 pages, only five focused on
guns.

Right after that report on Virginia Tech, I
realized that governments, large and small,
would probably do little to prevent mass
shootings. And my little butterfly folder wasn't
doing much either. I still wanted to do
something, but what? I was just another gun-
hater◉ just like half of this halfway gun-loving
country. But then I had an idea. I could start a
dialogue. What this nation needed was
grassroots conversation. Maybe if opposing
parties could talk◉and listen◉these
conversations would illuminate commonality.
We'd bring this commonality to our legislators
and they'd actually pass laws. Something

would be done then to prevent these senseless tragedies.

So I looked around for NRA-type folks to dialogue with, but found that harder than I realized. All my friends were gun control freaks. Even the Republican wing of my family drew the line at gun ownership. This was probably less ideological than practical though. The Jews that make up my family have trouble operating even the manicure scissors.

In the absence of real people to talk to, I began shouting at Fox News even more than usual. But I also began listening, trying to comprehend their stand on guns. The more I listened, the more I found that I agreed with them! What they were saying was exactly what my lefty friends were saying: Mentally ill people should not have access to guns.
In other words, commonality was possible!

The only problem was the database. I started thinking about the database…In order to keep guns out of the hands of crazies, there'd have to be some kind of database of anyone who's ever had a mental health diagnosis. You know how our therapists attach a DSM label to our amorphous neuroses so that insurance companies possibly will pay for the sessions that keep us slightly fucked up people sane?

That is exactly the kind of thing that would go in the database. Would all of Manhattan be in there? We're the sane ones! The people who should be there are the ones who shoot people in shopping mails, the ones who'd never in their not-right-minds see a shrink. And this is exactly what played out over the next months as more gunmen with no diagnoses went on killing sprees in Illinois, in Alabama, in California.

Obviously, weeding out wackos so they couldn't buy guns was not going to prevent these kinds of attacks. But that didn't mean there was no other opportunity for agreement among pro and anti-gun factions. To meet this challenge again (hopefully with more luck), I turned to Facebook, which I had recently joined. I know it's hard to believe there was ever a time before we were already on Facebook, but in early 2008 people, like myself, were just figuring out what to do with this platform. I tried posting gun control rants on my wall, and I got a lot of responses but, again, only from my friends, the Liberalati. Meanwhile, Fox News kept up their own rant and it was beginning to sound like this: To stop gun violence, we need more guns.

More guns?? Those people are such stupid doodoo heads, I thought, and I'm not ever going to be friends with them. To prove how stupid they were, my butterfly folder kept expanding. I'm talking about the gunman who stormed a city council meeting in Missouri, killing two police officers—who were armed. And then there was the four-year old girl in South Carolina who shot herself in the chest after snatching her grandmother's handgun at a Sam's Club. And what about the little boy who was shot near his Chicago apartment, his non-White face never appearing in Yahoo News? The members of his community went on TV begging America to get guns off the streets.

Two years after Virginia Tech, almost to the day, a gunman opened fire at an immigration center in Binghamton, NY, killing 13 people. America barely reacted. If one half of America couldn't really speak to the other half about stopping this shit, what was there to say?

Two more years passed, during which time lots of gun violence happened, but I had long ago stopped collecting stories. But then, just this past August, a gunman opened fire outside the Empire State Building, killing two and wounding nine. I used to live nearby; maybe that's why I got so shaken up. Right away, I went on Facebook and wrote:

Can anybody against gun control please explain to me how gun ownership could have helped today? I'm not being sarcastic.

Liberals, moderates, and conservatives chimed in this time, bouncing around their views⊚none of which were different than what any of us always says. However, everyone was respectful. "We did it," I thought. Here it was, the precondition for that elusive, but crucial commonality.

Then Charlie piped in. Charlie is someone I grew up, one of those old friends you were never really friends with that you feel compelled to connect with on Facebook. When I knew Charlie many years ago he was a skinny, nervous kid. However, he'd grown into a beefy gun rights advocate. Charlie responded to my post, saying: "Those cops," (he meant the ones at the Empire State Building) "they were terrible shooters." He then went on to praise his own marksmanship. In other words, in his mind, if he'd been in that crowd, he would have shot that gunman dead, avoiding other casualties. Suddenly, I realized that this way of thinking must be true for many pro-gun people. Maybe when they read these horrible Yahoo News stories, stuffing them into their own file folders, they're convinced the real reason this tragedy happened was because they weren't there to stop it. And stop it, they must. They really want to stop these kinds of shootings as much as I do. However, to my mind, they want to own a gun just so they can play cops and robbers all day long in their head.

And, yes Charlie, of course Charlie, you're the best shooter this side of Dodge, Kabul, and 34th street.

I want to mock Charlie's position. Too late. I already did. But we are four and a half years after Virginia Tech, and right after Newtown.

America is talking for real about gun violence and our government is finally poised to listen◎and to do something. Howeer, table where America finally reaches consensus about guns must be a table reserved for grown-ups◎from all sides. Let's bring to that table respect, deep listening, and empathy, as difficult as that is. Let this table be marked by real seriousness about solving this issue. But that doesn't mean this table's tablecloth can't be covered in butterflies.

THE GUNS IN MY PLAYS
An essay

By Tammy Ryan

[Tammy Ryan's plays have been performed across the United States and internationally. She won the 2012 ATCA Francesca Primus Prize for her play *Lost Boy Found in Whole Foods*, which was developed by the New Harmony Project, was a featured play at the National New Play Network's Showcase of New Plays and co-produced by Premiere Stages and Playwrights Theater of New Jersey (2010). Other plays include *Tar Beach, Lindsey's Oyster, Dark Part of the Forest, A Confluence of Dreaming, Baby's Blues, FBI Girl, In the Shape Of A Woman, The Music Lesson, The Boundary* and *Pig*. She is a Jane Chambers Playwriting Award honoree and her short play *Dry Cleaning the Soul* has been named as a finalist for the Heideman Award. Other honors include the American Alliance of Theater and Education's Distinguished Play Award, the Pittsburgh Cultural Trust's Creative Achievement Award, a Heinz Endowment's Creative Collaborative Residency and fellowships from Virginia Center for the Creative Arts, the Sewanee Writers Conference and Pennsylvania Council of the Arts. An artist in residence with the Western

Pennsylvania Young Writers Institute, Ryan teaches playwriting at Point Park University. She is serves as regional representative for the Dramatists Guild of America.
For more information: www.tammyryan.net.]

The blessing and the curse of the writer is her imagination. At every mention and at random moments of every day in those first few weeks after the shootings at Sandy Hook Elementary School, I would begin to imagine what occurred in those classrooms, what was waiting for the first responders, and for those children's parents. While I avoided most of the news on cable, I did venture onto facebook where I discovered some of my "friends" were anti gun control. I do not understand this position, so I started reading (and posting) all the articles I could find on gun legislation. I read some very cogent, practical and common sense responses as you would expect from New York Times columnist, Nicholas Kristof and others. And then I read Porochista Khakpour's essay Why Did Nancy Lanza Love Guns? In it, Khakpour describes her own personal journey of love, obsession and ultimately rejection of guns: guns made her feel safe, guns made her feel powerful, guns were sexy, guns were fun.

I met Khakpour when we were both fellows at the Sewanee Writers Conference in 2008. I see her standing at the podium, tall and beautiful, throwing back her long dark hair as she reads from her novel with a mischievous and joyful spirit, and now I can imagine her shooting a gun. I have never owned a gun, never touched a gun, never even ever seen a real gun. I don't share Khakpour's obsession, but the characters in my plays do. Not in all of them -- just the most successful ones, the ones that have been sanctioned by the powers that be as "good," the plays that receive professional development, multiple productions, get published and win awards. In each one of those plays a character either, has a gun, shoots a gun, is threatened by a gun, threatens someone else with a gun, is afraid of guns or is somehow traumatized by the violence of a gun.

This is a deeply disturbing revelation for me for several reasons. First, I don't think of myself as writing about guns. I think I'm writing about family, communication, the power of forgiveness and healing. But the presence of guns in my writing is undeniable. In my first play Pig, written straight out of grad school, a troubled sailor goes AWOL and takes his family hostage. He shoots his neighbor's dog (which was for audiences the most disturbing thing that happens) shoots his uncle and them himself. (note: I called it a comedy, okay, a black comedy) At the first talkback an audience member expressed disbelief that I'd written this play. The moderator chimed in, "Seriously, you look like you'd write something like Mary Poppins, where did this come from?" To be fair, at the time, even at thirty, I did look like I was twelve years old, but I was offended by the implication that a woman, even a seemingly innocent young woman couldn't write a play with what I then imagined as real world action in it. I wasn't going to be put in that woman ghetto box, thank you very much. After giving birth to my first daughter, however, my plays began to evolve. I knew I'd write different kinds of plays from that point on, and no matter how dark I'd go, always strive to "reach for the light." But, the guns kept coming back, emerging seemingly organically, in play after play.

Now, I am not a careful planner of my career. My ideas show up like orphaned babies on my doorstep that cry out in the cold until I cave in and let them in. Besides guns, there is also a lot of war (often as backdrop): the First Gulf War, Bosnia, the Hundred Years War, Sudan, Iraq. Once early in my career, my mother asked me "Why don't you write happy plays?" "I don't choose these subjects," I told her, "they choose me." I do enforce some practical parameters, like maybe don't put eleven characters in your plays unless you can double, but do I ever think, even subconsciously: better put a gun in your play if you want this one to get produced? Isn't there always an exchange, a feedback loop between artist and potential producer? The fact remains that it is my most commercially successful plays that are the ones with the guns. Marsha Norman said something to this effect in her article Not There Yet about gender equity in the theater. Says Norman, "People like the plays in which the women act like guys, talk like guys, wave guns around and threaten to kill each other... The critics have liked my "guy" plays—the ones with guns in them—and pretty much trashed the rest."

I'm not advocating for self censorship. I'm not saying never write about guns or violence, since writing about it is a way of standing up against it. As a student of mine said recently, "There are three hundred million guns in this country. We are clearly a gun culture. How can art not reflect that?" My husband is a good, gentle and kind man and his favorite movie is Pulp Fiction. Whenever it is on television (which is actually very often) he will stay up until two in the morning watching it again and again. "It's funny," he says. Is violence different when it's combined with humor? Does it make it more palpable? Or does it desensitize? I once wanted to walk out of a production of The Lieutenant of Inishman because I found the combination of butchery and comedy too much to take. Is it a matter of degree? I know I probably won't stop writing about violence despite these questions I have. In my current play, Soldier's Heart, a mother points a gun at her own child. It's integral to the action, to the theme and the whole point of the play, I'm not going to take that gun out of her hands. Despite Chekhov's rule, though, the gun does not go off, so maybe that's progress?

At Point Park University, where I teach, the Cinema and Digital Arts Department has a "no weapons" policy for its Introduction to Screenwriting and early production classes. It is explained as a way of providing parameters for screenplay assignments, but it also addresses a "production and liability/risk management issue," according to chair ,Nelson Chipman. "With such prevalence of weapons in current fictional shows, reality, news and gaming, we look for ways to help students create work that is more ingenuous…tasked with creating a story without weapons students actually get much more creative with violence and its repercussions." My students balked at this rule at first and found myriad ways to hide all manner of weapons in their scripts, reminding me of a story a friend told me about her toddler, who faced with his mother's strict no toy gun policy, bit his peanut butter sandwiches into the shape of pistols. But my insistence (points off for weapons) led them to discover that while guns can easily complicate a moment, create tension, lead to their climax, shock an audience, they are not necessary to good storytelling and in fact can limit the deep, surprising, complex and original conflicts that emerge in their work, finally. Without the guns, they were forced to imagine something new.

I read somewhere that after we dropped the bomb on Hiroshima, Bertolt Brecht went back and revised the plays that came before. He felt it wasn't the same world anymore, and that his plays, even the ones already written had to reflect that new reality. The massacre at Sandy Hook Elementary has done that to me, it's altered my view of reality. I'm not Bertolt Brecht, so I won't be revising those plays with guns in them, but going forward I'm going to be more mindful of what Brecht also said, "Art is not a mirror with which to reflect reality, but a hammer with which to shape it." The gift of imagination that the writer has been blessed with is sometimes a curse, but it can also be a tool. We as writers can reflect society or reshape it, but we also have the opportunity to more completely re-imagine it. And in that re-imagination, I believe, lies all of our hopes.

THE ARTIST AS ACTIVIST – TAKE IT TO THE STREET OR TO THE STAGE?

By
D.W. Gregory

D.W. Gregory writes in a variety of styles and genres, from historical drama to screwball comedy, but a recurring theme is the exploration of political issues through a personal lens. The New York Times called her "a playwright with a talent to enlighten and provoke" for her most produced play, RADIUM GIRLS (Playwrights Theatre of New Jersey), about dialpainters poisoned on the job in the 1920s. A resident playwright at New Jersey Rep, she received a Pulitzer nomination for the Rep's production of THE GOOD DAUGHTER, the story of a Missouri farm family struggling to adapt to rapid social change. Other plays include THE GOOD GIRL IS GONE (Playwrights Theatre) , a black comedy about maternal indifference; OCTOBER 1962 (NJ Rep), a Cold War era psychological thriller; and MOLUMBY'S MILLION (Iron Age Theatre Co.), a comedy about the boxer Jack Dempsey, which was nominated for the 2011 Barrymore Award for Outstanding New Play by the Theatre Alliance of Philadelphia. D.W. also writes frequently for youth theatre. Her play SALVATION ROAD, about a boy whose sister disappears into a fundamentalist church, was developed through New York University's Steinhardt New Plays for Young Audiences program and is slated for several productions in 2012-13. A member of the Dramatists Guild, a former national core member of The Playwrights' Center in Minneapolis, and a recent inductee into the League of Professional Theatre Women, Ms. Gregory is also founding member of the Playwrights Gymnasium, a process oriented workshop based in metro Washington, D.C. This interview originally appeared on DW Gregory's blog http://dwgregory.com/blog/the-artist-as-activist-take-it-to-the-street-or-the-stage/#.USbInKWTxEI.]

*

March on Washington for Gun Control, Jan. 26.

"When we stand together, we stand a chance"

On Jan. 26, 2013, after a month of planning that was kicked off by Arena Stage's artistic director, Molly Smith, the March on Washington for Gun Control took place—the first major public demonstration since the Sandy Hook shootings to demand a change in our national gun policy. I was in the thick of it, having helped (in a very small way) to assist the organizers and turning out to march and rally—one of more than 6,000 people who showed up that morning.

It was a first for me, to be in the midst of a movement, rather than at the edge of it, observing it. Up to this point in my life, the most I've ever done for any cause I've supported is to write a check. And while money helps, muscle is sometimes more important. So when Molly issued a call, I decided that it was time to do more than just lament a sorry situation. So I turned out to offer my limited skills at research and writing, helping collect as much information as I could on the issue and, with the help of my friend Cat, searching out the names of gun violence victims whose names were carried in silent protest down Constitution Avenue.

A view from within the crowd.

Later that afternoon, there was a demonstration of another kind at Georgetown University's Gonda Theatre—where Obie-winning playwright Caridad Svich, artistic director of NoPassport theatre alliance and press, had organized a Theatre Action for Gun Control in collaboration with Theatre J and interdisciplinary arts ensemble force/collision and Twinbiz. The presentation of short works included new pieces by Neil LaBute, Jennifer Maisel, Winter Miller, Matthew Paul Olmos, Svich, and others.

This juxtaposition of street theatre—which this march and rally surely was—and a theatre of protest in a traditional setting invites the question of what role art can play in responding to atrocity. The slaughter of those poor children and their teachers in Connecticut was so awful that any response at all seemed stunningly ineffectual. What can you say in response to such madness? And who is more crazy-- the gunman who took the lives of people totally unconnected to his personal hell--or the rest of us, who allow these conditions to persist and go so far as to argue--some of us--that our constitutional right to firearms trumps any reasonable effort to curtail their unlimited availability to individuals unfit to use them.

Are there moments when art has nothing to say? Or is it just that I have nothing to say; and for that reason decided to take up an action at Molly's invitation and do what little I could to make the point. Are there times when the only reasonable response is to put down the pen, take off the costume, and take to the street?

These are the questions I put to Caridad and her response is below the fold.

DW Gregory: How do you as an artist respond to an event like the massacre at Sandy Hook Elementary? Obviously you believe that art/theatre has something to say that is worthwhile--but my question is what? What can we possibly say or do that will make any difference to anyone in a culture so saturated with violence, so in love with the gun?

Caridad Svich: I am still a believer in the "every grain of sand" approach--that is, while a play or poem in and of itself may not effect immediate change, the effort to speak out and up, to raise the voice with power and feeling and artistry and passion, does matter. Otherwise, why are we artists? We make things, we throw light on our culture and its troubles because we do think it matters to someone somewhere down the pike, or we wouldn't even be in this art-making life to begin with. In the case of this specific theatre action for gun control it felt urgent and necessary to speak out with art in the moment and to this moment. After the Newtown massacre, I, too, personally as a citizen and artist, felt quite the same as you describe in your preface to these questions: helpless in the face of, hopeless, angry, etc. How can one not feel these things? But to not respond in some way either was equally troubling to me personally. I thought we must find a way to galvanize somehow as a country, as citizens, in any way we can to help make this a better, more just society. After the Columbine massacre, the issue of gun control was raised and all these years later, it still hangs in the balance. How many innocents need be killed before we try to effect some measure of change? The March that Molly Smith and Suzanne Blue Star Boy have organized is a visible sign, and because theatre work offers a space and place for reflection and gathering, I thought a theatre action could also be another sign to keep the voices raised, and not this "issue" fall by the wayside in our national debate yet again.

DW Gregory: We hear a lot of talk about "the cultural conversation" and how theatre needs to be part of it or drive it. But how do you address the fact that anyone who turns out for an evening of short works on gun control is already predisposed to be receptive to the idea of gun control? How do you reach the audience that would reject the notion out of hand? How do you see an evening of short plays having any impact at all---or is it really about allowing the artists to believe that they have done their "bit" by sounding off?

CS: Theatre is its own church and yes, the people who come may indeed be already part of the choir, as it were. Lobbyists know too who their "choirs" are and preach to them. If you study the history of art and efficacy-- especially guerrilla theatre, street theatre, and other forms of creative activism--there are many ways to go about trying to be part of the conversation and the wave of making a difference. I do not pretend that an evening of short works, again, will effect immediate change. Given the nature of the pieces, which reflect a range of responses--from prayers to meditations to calls for action--I think the writers selected in the curated evening offer plenty for an audience to consider about how gun violence has played a part in our lives. The artists who have come forth quite generously and have written pieces specifically for this event and are taking part as performers and organizers of this event are doing so because they believe in the power of community. Pure and simple. And especially in the power of being able to sit with tragedy in a space and reflect upon it and live with it (as we all do). One event does not heal these kinds of cultural wounds. But the space to reflect is crucial. I very much believe in the difference between making art that is targeted to change legislation, and the kind of work that is made to go beyond that. The March is, to my mind, very much in the spirit of calling on Washington to say "change in our gun laws must occur." It is a sign. Like holding up a placard. Like tagging a billboard. It is street action. But there is art-making too that can believe in the need for legislative change that is not made only with that kind of ambition--that instead, wishes to offer a related, empathetic space of intervention. The theatre action, and a simultaneous one occurring with NoPassport in collaboration with Pittsburgh PACT is free, and the artists who have taken part are not simply, as I have been in dialogue with them, behaving as if they are clicking a link or checking off a dutiful action on their checklist. We make theatre because we do think it matters, in its small, humble way. If the theatre action is staged in different cities after January 26, perhaps we will discover different ways to wear both hats--the art for immediate efficacy hat, and the art for longstanding cultural soul-work and reparation hat--simultaneously. One step at a time.

DW Gregory: What role do you believe the arts have played in contributing to a culture of violence? The NRA blames video games and Hollywood films--without mentioning what the gun industry has paid for product placement--but is there any truth to the charge? What soul searching must we as storytellers do, when "conflict" is the essential element of drama? Has violence become an easy out for lazy storytellers--and if so, what is the answer?

CS: When I teach playwriting and creative writing, the representation of violence onstage and in prose, film and other narrative and non-narrative art genres is, by nature, a necessary point of discussion, as much as it is when I make work and/or view/witness work made by others. What is the artist's obligation and/or moral duty when representing violence? A thorny, complicated question that has riddled authors and theorists for centuries, from the ancient Greek dramatists on down. Is "conflict" hardwired in our storytelling because as human beings we are "hardwired" for it? Is the representation of violence a necessary condition, then, of storytelling? The storytelling adage goes: If you pull out a gun in a play, then at some point you are going to have to use it. But what if you don't? And what if a gun never appears on stage? is there an easy answer here? Do we say "place all violence offstage, and let the messenger tell us what happened?" Or do we let Gloucester gets his eyes blinded right in front of us? What does the "showing" of violence mean for the audience who receives it?

In theatre, I think, the representation of violence, when used with judgment and clarity and sophistication by an artist, can be a necessary tool for storytelling - and here I include emotional, psychological as well as physical violence. Can you imagine The Bacchae, for example, without the raging bacchants? Theatre is a visceral medium. It is, in part, about awakening the senses. In theatre, in live performance, violence as signifier carries a different change than in the plastic mediums like film. One blow from one character to another in theatre can send a charge through an audience - that is not titillating but rather calling into question moral actions.

In film and video, because of the very nature of the medium, its plasticity, I would argue, the "ease" of violence and its mechanics - blowing up cities, shoot-outs, etc. - becomes often mere "choreography." It can encourage desensitization in an audience member. How many characters does one see get killed every week on TV and film, for instance? The same desensitization can apply to how audiences watch graphic news events on TV and online. The "wars" that are "over there" become "theoretical" and the killed "mere" collateral damage.

Theatre's job, in part, in its role as part of civic engagement, is to remind the audience , should it choose to do so within the telling of a chosen story, that, in effect, it is not something toward which one should be (desensitized). Are there lazy storytellers that resort to the use of violence? Yes. But there always have been. Are multinationally-financed Hollywood films and videogames to blame? I don't believe in censorship, but I do believe in, again, the artist's moral responsibility. You have a choice when you make something in a free society. You choose which stories you wish to tell and why and how.

In many cases, shall we say, in the case of B and C Hollywood filmmaking, we are talking about product-makers and merchants. So, how do you begin to have a dialogue with people who feel that all they are doing is making product to fulfill a market need? Do you ask the product-maker to consider their moral action or the lure of the $? I think fundamentally this is the question quite often. Are you willing as a product-maker to not make the $ in order to help change the kind of content (and perhaps then affect the level of desensitization) viewed by the potential buyer? Are you willing to stop business as usual?

DW Gregory: I will ruminate on that question in another post---but that, as she observes, really is the fundamental issue here. Where do we draw the line in what we are willing to do for money? The gun lobby has decided that its profits trump public safety and all common sense and it has poured millions into a public propaganda campaign to convince Americans that their fundamental right to self defense and self determination is threatened by people who think that sub-machine guns really have no place in civilized society.

What ought to be a no-brainer is looking increasingly like a very tough sell on Capitol Hill.

So perhaps the question is not so much what to say, but how to say it in a way that can capture the attention of people otherwise disposed to ignore you. That's a question playwrights struggle with as a matter of course---but when it comes to the rot at the core of the American psyche, it is an even greater challenge. For I sense that one reason this debate is in the spin cycle is that the problem, fundamentally, is not guns.

It is self-delusion.

Actors and theatre-makers who took part in the January 26, 2013 NoPassport Gun Control Theatre Action in Washington D.C. in collaboration with Theater J and force/collision and Twinbiz were:

Frank Britton is a native Washingtonian, alumnus and faculty member of the National Conservatory of Dramatic Arts, and a two-time Helen Hayes Award nominee in the category of Outstanding Ensemble, Resident Play, and is currently appearing in The Minotaur (Rorschach Theatre). Recent appearances include Shape (DC World Premiere and NYC Premiere at La MaMa ETC--force/collision, Core Ensemble/founding member); Marathon '33 (The American Century Theater); The Bacchae, Les Justes (WSC Avant Bard--Acting Company Member--nearly a dozen productions, including the titular role in Richard III); and has also appeared in productions with many area theatres including Arena Stage, Round House Theatre, Synetic Theater, Theater Alliance, SCENA Theatre, Constellation Theatre Co., Forum Theatre, Spooky Action Theater, and regionally with the Virginia Shakespeare Festival and Baltimore Shakespeare Festival.

Sarah Elizabeth Ewing, a force/collision member, has trained in Washington DC and Los Angeles. Through her work with force/collision and The Rude Guerrilla Theater Company (Orange County, CA) she has been fortunate to perform in the world and US premiers of The Nautical Yards (Ensemble), The Sacred Geometry of S&M Porn (Margaret), and San Diego (Amy). Regional credits include: NYC: Shape (Ensemble); LA/OC: HAMLETMACHINE (Hanged Woman), The Municipal Abattoir (The Girl), The Gift (Janie), Bus Stop (Elma), and A Lie of the Mind (Sally).

Dexter Hamlett, in 2012 appeared in Erik Ehn's, Shape, produced by Force Collision at La Mamma ECT. As well as Factory 449.s The Ice Child, an urban horror, and a fortunate trip to London to work for the first time in 30 years with Isolte Avila and David Bower in, Signdance Collective's, New Gold. He began the year working on the Heritage O'Neill, Moon for the Misbegotten as Phil Hogan. The body of his work on the west coast, he studied theater at Cal Arts and is truly mad.

Mark Krawczyk is an actor, a teacher, and an advocate for gun control. You can learn more about him at www.markkrawczyk.weebly.com.

Jocelyn Kuritsky has performed in and/or developed shows with 13P, PS 122, The Chocolate Factory, Clubbed Thumb, Dixon

Place, Ensemble Studio Theatre, The Greenpoint Division, HERE Arts Center, La MaMa E.T.C., the Lark Play Development Center, Les Freres Corbusier, Little Theatre, MCC Theater, the Museum of Modern Art, New Dramatists, New Georges, The New Group, New York Stage and Film, New York Theatre Workshop, Page 22, Primary Stages, The Public, Rattlestick Playwrights Theater, Red Bull Theater, Shelby Company, Soho Rep., SPACE on Ryder Farm, Target Margin, & Working Theater. She also performs regularly with her critically acclaimed theater company, Woodshed Collective, where she is a core member and the actor in residence. Her film credits include Peace After Marriage, opposite Louise Lasser, and The Girl Next Door. She has assisted directors Trip Cullman, Kip Fagan, Carl Forsman, Will Frears, Victor Maog, Ian Morgan, John Gould Rubin, & Michael Sexton, as well as collaborated with musician Duncan Sheik. www.jocelynkuritsky.com

John Moletress is founding director of force/collision. OFF-OFF BROADWAY: La MaMa ETC: Shape. REGIONAL: Stages Repertory Theatre: Mistakes Were Made; Steel River Playhouse: Pippin; The Crucible. DC AREA: The Nautical Yards, Magnificent Waste (World Premiere), The Saint Plays, Airswimming, 4.48 Psychosis (Capital Fringe Festival Award winner), What A Stranger May Know, Collapsing Silence, Foreign Tongue (World Premiere). OTHER: Founding Director, force/collision; Co-Founder of Helen Hayes Awards' John Aniello Award winning Factory 449; Kennedy Center/American College Theatre. Festival educator/respondent; 2012 Mayor's Arts Award finalist; JohnMoletress.com

Karin Rosnizeck is a founding member force/collision and performed in SHAPE and The Nautical Yards. Other roles: Magdalena Sanger (Marathon '33), Nanni (The Ice Child with Factory 449), Mrs. Winsley/ Nurse in Stop Kiss, title role in The Gnädiges Fräulein, Countess Geschwitz in Lulu, Camille Claudel in The Sculptress. She will next appear in the silliest play ever written - The Little Theatre of the Green Goose -with Ambassador Theater. Karin has also worked as dialect coach and script consultant for German plays (Studio Theater, Theater J) and translated Cold Country by Swiss playwright Reto Finger for Zeitgeist. She holds an M.A. in English and French literature and believes in soft power.

Sue Jin Song is a founding member of force/collision. She has numerous film, television, and theatrical credits (locally and regionally). She received her MFA in acting from NYU's Tisch School of the Arts. Sue Jin is gratified to be taking part in this evening's readings. It's nights like this that made her want to be an artist. She hopes this night brings healing, provokes thought, strengthens community, and inspires action. These deaths will not be in vain.

Howard Wahlberg is a former Director of Marketing for Arena Stage. Selected previous credits: No Rules Theatre Company's Stop Kiss, directed by Holly Twyford, and Suicide, Incorporated; The Gaming Table (u/s, Folger Theatre), Time Stands Still (u/s Studio Theatre), Cry for the Gods, (Capital Fringe Festival). Howard studied the Meisner technique with Kathryn Gately at Mason Gross School of the Arts, as well as improvisation, pantomime, and clowning with Tanya Belov, Ronlin Foreman, Steve Smith, Glen "Frosty" Little, and Lou Jacobs at Ringling Brothers and Barnum & Bailey's Clown College.

Laura Zam Laura Zam is a writer/performer specializing in one-person plays. Venues: The Public Theater, EST, Woolly Mammoth, and others nationally and internationally. Her newest play Married Sex was recently commissioned by Theater J. Awards include Tennessee Williams Fellowship, Soros Foundation grant, and Artist Fellowship

(DCCAH). Laura has published in Time Out, Velvet Magazine, and Monologues for Women, by Women II, among others. She's also worked with trauma survivors all over the world, including teens from the Middle East and wounded veterans. She has an M.F.A. in Playwriting from Brown University. LauraZam.com.

Rachel Zampelli is an actress based in Washington, DC. Her most recent work includes Dying City (Signature Theatre) and Bloody, Bloody Andrew Jackson (The Studio Theatre 2ndStage). Rachel received her BA in Theater at Santa Clara University. She is looking forward to finishing up this season at Signature Theatre playing Meg in Beth Henley's Crimes of the Heart, directed by Aaron Posner and Marta in Stephen Sondheim's Company, directed by Eric Schaeffer.

NoPassport

NoPassport is a Pan-American theatre alliance & press devoted to live, virtual and print action, advocacy and change toward the fostering of cross-cultural diversity in the arts with an emphasis on the embrace of the hemispheric spirit in US Latina/o and Latin-American theatre-making.

NoPassport Press' Dreaming the Americas Series and Theatre & Performance PlayTexts Series promotes new writing for the stage, texts on theory and practice and theatrical translations.

Series Editors: Tony Adams, Mead Hunter, Jorge Huerta, Randy Gener, Otis Ramsey-Zoe, Stephen Squibb, Caridad Svich

Advisory Board: Daniel Banks, Amparo Garcia-Crow, Maria M. Delgado, Randy Gener, Elana Greenfield, Christina Marin, Antonio Ocampo Guzman, Sarah Cameron Sunde, Saviana Stanescu, Tamara Underiner, Patricia Ybarra

NoPassport is a sponsored project of Fractured Atlas, a non-profit arts service organization. Contributions in behalf of [Caridad Svich & NoPassport] may be made payable to Fractured Atlas and are tax-deductible to the extent permitted by law.

For online donations go directly to https://www.fracturedatlas.org/donate/2623

Made in the USA
Lexington, KY
27 October 2013